Dealer's choice

The dealer hit the ground first, landing in a heap of flailing arms and legs, grunting heavily as Clint knocked all the air from his lungs by falling squarely on top of his body.

Another shot echoed through the saloon, but this time it didn't come from the man Clint was watching. Instead, it came from somewhere closer to Kieffer's poker table which set off yet another wave of thundering footsteps.

Clint's world shook and rattled around him. His ears rang from the gunshots and his heart thumped brutally inside his rib cage. Fighting through the adrenaline that coursed through his veins, he pushed off the floor with one hand, tossing his body back so that it lay completely on top of the poor, squashed dealer.

All Clint could see was the gunman turning around, tracking Clint's movements with wild, staring eyes . . .

OUTLAW LUCK

J. R. ROBERTS

JOVE BOOKS, NEW YORK

This is a work of fiction. Names, characters, places, and incidents either are the product of the author's imagination or are used fictitiously, and any resemblance to actual persons, living or dead, business establishments, events, or locales is entirely coincidental.

OUTLAW LUCK

A Jove Book / published by arrangement with the author

PRINTING HISTORY
Jove edition / March 2002

All rights reserved.
Copyright © 2002 by Robert J. Randisi.
This book, or parts thereof, may not be reproduced in any form without permission.
For information address: The Berkley Publishing Group,
a division of Penguin Putnam Inc.,
375 Hudson Street, New York, New York 10014.

Visit our website at
www.penguinputnam.com

ISBN: 0-515-13267-5

A JOVE BOOK®
Jove Books are published by The Berkley Publishing Group,
a division of Penguin Putnam Inc.,
375 Hudson Street, New York, New York 10014.
JOVE and the "J" design
are trademarks belonging to Penguin Putnam Inc.

PRINTED IN THE UNITED STATES OF AMERICA

10 9 8 7 6 5 4 3 2 1

ONE

Clint Adams had been meaning to get out of New Mexico for some time.

The funny thing about the place was that the longer he stayed, the less he tried to go anywhere else. Sure, he knew he'd eventually move on just like he moved on from nearly every other state in the Union, but for the moment New Mexico was kind of growing on him.

Maybe it was something in the fresh, warm air that blew down over the desert sands like a gentle breath from the clouds overhead. Or perhaps it was the glorious purples and reds of dusk that were so vastly different from the vibrant yellows and orange of dawn. There were sunsets and sunrises in every other state, but there just seemed to be something different about the ones he'd been seeing over the past month or so.

Something more inspiring.

In fact, Clint had been working his way slowly back toward West Texas with the idea of going back to Labyrinth to check in with his more familiar stomping grounds. But things always had a way of coming up along the way, so Clint decided to roll with them and go wherever the breeze took him. After all, Labyrinth wasn't going anywhere.

Riding at a leisurely pace from Arizona into New Mexico,

Clint found that it did his soul some good to just wander for a bit. After all, there was something indescribably wonderful about simply pointing Eclipse in one direction, any direction, and letting the Darley Arabian stallion roam.

The young horse had a knack for sniffing out good campsites and the occasional town at those times when both he and his rider preferred the comforts of civilization over the embrace of a starry sky. After all of this time on the trail, Clint almost felt as though he could simply think about where he wanted to go and Eclipse would take him there. Of course, it helped that both of them never decided on a destination until it was within sight.

They were riding slowly on the western edge of a vast stretch of desert. Spread out to the east was miles of rocky terrain that looked as though it hadn't seen a good rain since before Clint had been born. The surface of the boulders was parched and cracked as an old man's cheek, laying beneath the swirling sand like an animal doing its best to escape the sun's rays.

Clint had been through a town only a couple of days ago that was one of the lesser-known stops on the local gambling circuit. The nation's card players drifted in flocks from state to state, town to town, searching for the big games and going wherever the money was. Sometimes they swooped down onto a certain place like a bunch of locusts in black suits and string ties, drinking all the whiskey and fleecing each other for every cent they could grab.

After that, they moved on to the next place, anted up in the next game and started the whole process over again.

While Clint wasn't exactly a part of the gambler's circuit, he did spend more than his fair share of sleepless nights staring at cards through the smoky haze of crowded saloons. In fact, he'd been on something of a streak over the last week and eventually found out that he'd stumbled upon a rich source of gaming revenue in a little place called Three Doors, New Mexico.

Three Doors didn't have much more than that inside its limits, and the biggest building of them all was the saloon. Beyond that particular door, Clint had found several poker players who had no intentions of leaving their spots until they'd either taken every chip that touched the table or lost everything they owned.

Although Clint was no thief, his luck had been running good enough to make him feel as though he was stealing those men's cash right out from under them. Being professionals, however, they took their losses as graciously as their wins and even asked if Clint would be moving on to White Sands for a series of high-stakes games that would be taking place over the next several days.

He had nothing else to do, it was a big town where he could spend some time in a nicer hotel with some better food and the saloons would be filled with gamblers aching to give Clint a run for his money at games that could quite possibly reach epic proportions. The more he thought about it, the less Clint thought he could lose in the deal.

And, like so many other famous disasters, going to White Sands sounded like a good idea at the time.

But that kind of insight wouldn't come for a while yet. Right now, all Clint was concerned about was getting to White Sands before all the good rooms were taken up by gamblers who'd arrived ahead of him. The biggest thing on Clint's mind at that particular moment was what he might be able to get for dinner. After all, baked beans and coffee around a glowing fire might have had a certain charm, but it was a long way from a thick-cut steak and a fat piece of pie for dessert.

White Sands loomed in front of him like a boxy mirage on the horizon. Another hour's ride and he would be close enough to smell the food from one of the town's restaurants and hear the sounds of a saloon at full capacity.

He wasn't more than a few miles outside of the town's limits when a stagecoach rumbled toward him from the northwest. It was a big carriage being pulled by a team of six horses that made the ground rattle with the pounding of their feet. When the coach passed him by, Clint suddenly felt as though he'd crossed a line separating him from the solitude of the trail and civilization.

No longer was he the only soul around for as far as he could see. At once, the sounds of a busy community assaulted his ears and the sight of a hundred intersecting lives filled his eyes. People walked next to and around each other, bumping into some while carefully avoiding others like ants on a hill moving around with crumbs on their backs.

Clint found the livery and put Eclipse up for the night, instructing the stable boy to be careful with the stallion and treat him to a generous helping of greens. He would check in with Eclipse tomorrow, but for a change, right now all Clint wanted was to be around some company that had less than four legs.

He strode down the street with his saddlebags over his shoulder, soaking in the atmosphere of the town while also keeping his eye out for a place to stay. By the looks of things, plenty of gamblers had already found their way to town and were making themselves comfortable.

Plenty of well-dressed men stood outside the saloons, nursing cigars and stretching their legs. Clint knew from experience exactly which muscles tended to pinch and tense after sitting at a game for most of a day. Judging by the expressions on a few of the faces, there were plenty of winners in town as well, strutting from bar to bar with women on their arms who laughed at everything they said and batted their eyelashes whenever their benefactor looked their way.

Yes indeed, Clint thought. This was going to be one hell of a stay.

TWO

The White Sands Inn was as good a place to stay as any others that Clint passed on his walk through town. It looked clean and the prices were reasonable. But what it all boiled down to was the fact that all Clint was really looking for was a place to store his gear and sign his name so he could get down to the serious business of gambling.

In fact, Clint barely remembered much about the place besides his room number. When his senses snapped back onto full alert, he was standing at the end of the saloon district, listening to the inviting sound of pianos being played and rowdy voices being raised. The last vestiges of sunlight were just beginning to fade when Clint picked one of the saloons and stepped inside.

As an afterthought, he looked over his shoulder at the large window on the saloon's facing wall and read the letters stenciled onto the glass. Spelled out backwards in ornate, blocky script were the words SPLIT HITCH SALOON. The inside was taken up primarily by a row of card tables set up in front of a large stage. Although there were no performers at the moment, he could spot several brightly dressed showgirls making the rounds throughout the crowd. They circulated among drinkers and gamblers alike, stirring up the men until the smiles became a little too wide on their faces, and then moving on to the next.

One in particular caught Clint's eye. She walked across the loose floorboards in an impressive display of grace and agility, considering that she was perched on boots with two-inch heels. The polished leather held onto her legs all the way up to her knees, which she displayed every now and then by turning with a flourish and causing her red-and-black skirts to billow out around her. Her skin looked especially pale in comparison to the colors she wore, giving her flesh a soft, touchable quality that wasn't lost on the men she passed who all tried to snake their hands around her waist or even sneak them onto her rounded bottom.

But she danced away from their ham-handed attempts with a twirl and a smile, waving her finger playfully at them while strutting right over to start the entire process again. Clint watched her work, admiring the way her dark brown hair danced around her face and the way her perfectly tailored dress hugged her curves as though it was a living thing wrapping itself around every inch of her that it could reach.

If ever Clint could be jealous of something made of sequins and silk, this was that time.

Suddenly, she flipped her hair over her shoulder and turned to look in Clint's direction. She scanned the crowd for a second before settling her eyes onto him as though she could feel his gaze sweeping over her body. The corners of her red-painted lips turned up in a sly grin as she slowly brushed a hand down her hip.

Clint was about to accept the invitation she'd been sending him when he heard a voice coming from directly in front of him that seemed to drift out of empty air.

"Help you with something, mister?" it said.

Clint blinked once and then again before realizing that he was standing at the end of the bar. Somehow, he'd wound up with one foot up on the railing that bordered the bottom of the entire bar, one of his hands resting idly on the finely polished surface. It became clear at that moment just how accustomed to saloons he truly was. Without even paying attention to where he was going, he'd walked in and made himself at home.

Then again, it sure beat the hell out of walking into a pole like most others when they weren't looking where they were going.

"Mister?" came the voice again. "Are you all right?"

Clint shook the cobwebs out of his head and spotted the squat bartender standing staring at him with wide, jittery eyes. The man was shaped like so many of the boulders that Clint had passed while riding through the desert. His arms and legs hung off of the rest of his body like stubby afterthoughts formed from whatever scrap pieces the man's creator had lying around.

Although obviously muscled, the bartender carried most of his weight around his middle, which he tried without success to hide by wearing a large apron tied around his waist. One of his eyes was slightly off center and stared at a point over Clint's head and to the left. Once Clint met his gaze, the barkeep smiled broadly, displaying a set of randomly placed teeth that might very well have been on the receiving end of a mule's kick.

"You look like you've had a long day," the barkeep said amiably. "How about starting off with something to wake you up?"

"Yeah. That's probably a good idea."

"Especially after getting a nice eyeful of Alison, huh?"

Reflexively, Clint's eyes darted toward the showgirl on the other side of the room. She'd already hopped onto the lap of an older man sitting at one of the poker tables and was wrapping her arms around the lucky fellow's neck.

"Don't feel bad," the barkeep said. "You wouldn't be the first man to lose his senses soon after laying eyes on that one. Hell, I work here and sometimes it's hard for me to keep the glasses from sliding right out of my hands."

Clint shook his head and finally felt as though every part of him was present and accounted for. When he looked in front of him, he found a cup of steaming coffee waiting to be drunk. He leaned over it and extended his hand. "Much obliged. My name's Clint."

The bartender's hand wrapped around Clint's with room to spare. The crooked smile returned and was accompanied by a curt nod. "I'm Ben. Are you here for the cards?"

"Sure enough. Looks like you see a lot of gamblers around here."

"Only lately. I don't know what it is, but in the space of a few weeks we've gone from a decent gaming business to a landslide. Believe it or not, this here place was almost torn down due to lack of interest just before the heat got turned up. Now the owner's looking for more places to stash his money."

Raising his glass, Clint said, "Well, here's to hoping that I have that same problem before too long."

Ben produced a shot glass from beneath the bar, splashed some whiskey into it and downed it all in one gulp. With another wave of his hand, the glass was gone and the spot he'd made was wiped off the top of the bar. "I'll drink to that . . . even though I probably shouldn't while on the job."

The coffee was hot and strong, which was exactly what saloon coffee was supposed to be. Leave it to restaurants to brew rich, tasty blends. Saloons served coffee to energize gamblers and wake up drunks long enough for them to stay upright until they made it out the door. Already, Clint's eyes were brightening and he could feel the fatigue from the trail leaking out of him.

THREE

"So when does the action start around here?" Clint asked.

Ben turned to look over his shoulder at a small clock that hung on the wall over the shelf of bottles behind the bar. "Alison starts her show along with all the other girls in a few minutes. They do a few numbers at the top of every hour."

"Actually, I was talking about the poker games . . . but thanks all the same." As a matter of fact, hearing that the showgirl would be performing soon temporarily put cards out of Clint's mind. Once again, he looked over to where she'd been, but Alison had already moved on and was lost among the growing crowd of milling bodies.

Nodding slowly, Ben refilled Clint's coffee and nudged him on the shoulder. "I thought I'd go for the safe bet on that question. The way you were looking at her, I'd say you would've gotten around to asking me that sooner or later."

Clint laughed despite himself. "I can't exactly argue you on that one."

Ben leaned forward with his elbows resting on the bar. "You see that dandy sitting over there with the schoolteacher spectacles?"

Clint turned around to look at where Ben was pointing. At first, he couldn't see much besides the crowd, which churned and swayed as one like the rolling waves of the ocean. Eventually, he picked out individual tables amid the chaos and then he could finally make out a few specific faces.

One of those faces belonged to a man who looked to be in his mid- to late-fifties wearing a pair of glasses that sat on the bridge of his nose and were connected to his collar by a thick black ribbon. A thick clump of fluffy gray hair made a ring around the back of his head while leaving a large area on top of his scalp smooth and clean as a polished egg. Although he conversed with the others at his table, the older man seemed somehow removed from them. An air of haughty superiority hung over his head.

"I see him," Clint said.

"If you're playing five card draw, then that's where you'll want to start. Old man Kieffer has a lot of money to his name and doesn't mind dropping a hundred or two some nights."

"Any reason why you'd single him out?"

"Just trying to help. That's all. He just told me to send over anyone interested in a full night of cards. He's already got plenty to add to the pot, and you seemed like a good enough fella. Thought I'd do you a favor." Lowering his voice to a conspiratorial whisper, Ben added, "And trust me . . . it is a favor."

Clint was automatically suspicious whenever he was on the receiving end of tips like this one. Usually, these types of leads meant that either the person doing the leading was getting some kind of kickback or that the game was a trap set up for unsuspecting rubes with a lot of money to lose and not enough sense to keep away from con artists.

But there was something that told Clint right away that Kieffer's game was not just a con man's trap. It told him that even if there were cheats at that table, they were either the dumbest ones in the country or were simply taking time off to enjoy an honest game for a change.

In fact . . . that something was a someone.

"Is that who I think it is?" Clint said, more to himself than the bartender.

Ben squinted his eyes and shrugged again. "I can't see what you're talking about."

"That man right there," Clint said, trying hard not to point any fingers. "Sitting two chairs over on Mister Kieffer's left."

"Oh, you know Mister Garrett?"

"Do I know Pat Garrett? Yeah. I think I may have heard his name somewhere before." Or seen his face in the papers several hundred times.

Clint set a few coins on the bar to cover his tab and took his coffee with him as he made his way across the room. While sidestepping all the gamblers, dancers and drunks that moved around him, Clint could only think about the man he'd happened to spot at Mr. Kieffer's card table.

Pat Garrett was best known as the man who'd put an end to one of the most famous outlaws in history: Billy the Kid. Rumors and controversy still swirled around the manner in which Garrett, acting as sheriff of Lincoln County, shot and killed the nationally known and revered Kid. Some even went so far as to make out the Kid to be some kind of hero rather than a cold-blooded killer and desperate fugitive.

Those same critics called Garrett a traitor who had at one time been a friend to William Bonney, only to turn on the Kid when enough money was dangled in front of him. Of course, Clint knew better than to mind critics like those.

Most of the time, those critics hadn't even fired a gun and couldn't comprehend what it was like to be on the wrong end of a weapon being held by someone the likes of William Bonney. As far as Clint knew, Pat Garrett was a man who had a job to do and eventually got it done. Beyond that, it was hard to say since he'd never really met the lawman.

All of this went through Clint's head in the time it took him to maneuver his way through the crowd and step up to one of the empty spots across from Mister Kieffer. Clint set his coffee down and pulled out a chair. "Mind if I sit down?" he asked.

Mr. Kieffer regarded Clint the way a king might glance at one of his kitchen servants. In fact, he looked so far down his nose that it was doubtful he could see much else besides the pointy end of it. After what seemed like an unnaturally long pause, Kieffer waved his hand toward Clint and nodded regally. "Go ahead and sit. That is, as long as you don't mind losing your money."

"Mind?" Clint said, while plastering on his best innocent expression. He reached into his jacket's inside pocket and removed a small stack of bills. Setting the cash on the table, he grinned at the old man. "Why, I insist on it."

Garrett turned in his chair to look at Clint head-on. His sharp eyes were somewhat hooded, but still managed to absorb every last detail that could be seen. His mouth looked more like a deep incision beneath a bushy graying mustache, turned down at the edges in a serious frown. After regarding Clint for no more than a second or two, his eyes narrowed slightly.

It was at that moment that Clint knew what it felt like to be in the lawman's sights.

"Do you know this man, Mister Garrett?" Kieffer asked.

"Not yet," he said while raising up from his chair in a show of respect. Extending his hand across the table, he added, "Please join us, Mister . . ."

"Adams," Clint said.

Garrett nodded. "I figured as much. I've heard you were in the area and was hoping to catch sight of you before you moved on. It's been a while since a man of your caliber has been in these parts."

"I'm just here for cards."

"Of course. Shall we begin?"

Clint nodded, pulled in his chips and got ready to test his own luck against a legend.

FOUR

"Will you look at that murderous son of a bitch?"

Three men sat around a table near the back of the Split Hitch Saloon. Although they were facing the stage, their attention was focused on anything but the dancing girls that had begun to prance into the spotlight. The figures huddled together in the darkness, speaking in quick whispers as if anyone else could hear them over the chaotic noise that filled the saloon all the way up to the rafters.

The one who'd just asked the question glared intently over at one of the poker tables closer to the stage. His eyes lanced straight through anyone who passed into his field of vision to bore directly into the skull of one of the faraway players.

"Which one you talking about?" asked one of the other men at the table. "Garrett, or the one that just sat down?"

"Take yer pick. I ain't got much use for either of 'em."

Mick Drezdev sat hunched over his drink like a troll protecting his turf beneath the local bridge. By the age of thirty-six, he'd already begun to develop a stooped-over posture that made him carry himself as though he was constantly cowering from some unseen threat. In response to the poor hand that nature had dealt him, he stared out at the world in constant challenge, waiting for someone to look at him the wrong way or say the wrong thing.

Rather than deal with Drezdev and his foul temper, the part of White Sands that recognized him simply turned the other way and made a point not to speak to him, the idea being to simply keep any matches away from an open powder keg. The result was just another thing for the oddly shaped man to be pissed off about.

The only people that didn't mind sharing Drezdev's company were Tom Carlyle and William Krow. Of those two, Carlyle was closest to Drezdev in size, if not demeanor.

Tom Carlyle stood a good six inches below most men, but made up for it by being nearly twice as wide as them. His shoulders were so broad, they resembled end tables on either side of his face. Since his chest barreled out so far, it caused him to walk with his arms thrust back and his chin held up. The muscles lining his forearms were thick, knotted masses that strained the sleeves of his shirt.

In contrast, Will Krow looked like a blade of grass to Carlyle's tree. His eyes were dull and hooded, set close together on a face that didn't have much room to spare. Although taller than most folks, he was built as though he'd been stretched out like a thin piece of taffy. But there was something behind those close-set eyes that betrayed a whole lot going on inside. It was something that seemed to be watching his friends just as closely as he watched everyone else. And it was that something that made any observer wonder just what the hell he was planning that he wasn't ready to talk about yet.

For the moment, the three men sat around their table and scrutinized the poker players at the other end of the room. The lights around the stage flared up a bit as the rest of the room was put into temporary shadow. A pair of pianos started playing and the rest of the showgirls that had been making their rounds throughout the saloon hopped to their feet and began running for the stage.

"You know who that is talking to Garrett?" Krow asked.

Drezdev nodded. "Sure do. We heard about Clint Adams making his way through Arizona. It was only a matter of time before he came here. Probably came to get in on some of the gambling like the rest of them fancy-dressed leaches."

Squinting and leaning forward slightly, Carlyle peered into the darkness. "How can you tell that's really him?"

"I can tell," Drezdev said with a scowl. "That's the Gunsmith. I'd stake everything I got on it."

The clatter of high heels on floorboards approached their table like an oncoming train. Before either of the men bothered to turn and look, they were overtaken by a flurry of skirts and brown hair as one of the showgirls began dancing around and plopped down onto Carlyle's lap.

"What could you boys be talking about that's better than watching the show?" Alison asked while wrapping her arms playfully around Carlyle's neck.

Drezdev turned his head so slowly that Alison swore she could hear his neck creaking. "Get yer ass out of here, woman," he snarled, "before I put my boot in it."

Not even the first trace of fear came to Alison's face. In fact, she looked more like she was trying to keep from saying something else just to prod Drezdev even further. Whether or not any of the men noticed her lack of shaking in response to the other man's threat, Alison curled up on Carlyle's lap and held on as though she was about to fall off.

"You won't let him hurt me, will you?" she said in a playfully frightened voice.

Carlyle's hands came around her waist and lifted her up without much effort. He kept them there even after moving her aside and setting her onto her feet. "Best for you to move on. But come back later . . . I've got something for you."

Winking subtly, Alison shifted her lips slightly while bending down to whisper in his ear. "I'll see you later, handsome. Just make sure you're ready."

Watching her for as long as he could, Carlyle kept his eyes glued to the showgirl's backside until she was swallowed up by the crowd. He was brought back to reality by the insistent snapping of Drezdev's fingers.

"Stop thinking with yer dick and pay attention," the gnarled Russian said. "We can't have the likes of Clint Adams hanging around that man. Not now."

Krow held his whiskey glass in one hand and stared down

at the murky brown liquid. "Maybe we should just put off the plan until Adams leaves. It would be a whole lot easier than trying to fight him off."

"And when is that?" Drezdev grunted. "When will he leave?"

"Probably with the rest of the gamblers. They won't stay forever."

"Can you guarantee that they'll be gone in time for us to do our job?"

"No."

Drezdev stared at Krow with blatant contempt burning in his eyes. "And when will these gamblers leave, anyway? Do you even know that much?"

Turning away from his whiskey so he could look down at Drezdev, Krow bit his tongue before he said something to pull the conversation completely away from business and provoke the smaller man any further. He shook his head rather than say anything at all.

When Drezdev laughed, it sounded more like the snort of a rooting boar. "I didn't think so. And all this time, you had us fooled into thinking you were so goddamn smart. What the hell good are you?"

Krow wasn't offended by Drezdev's words. In fact, he wasn't expecting anything less than what he'd heard. Most of the Russian's attitude was soaked up from the bottle he was always draining, as was a good portion of his courage. Another thing Krow expected was a favorable response when he said, "I am smart enough to know a way to get Adams out of our way tonight. And I'm smart enough to know how to get rid of another little problem as well."

"Ahhh," Drezdev said as a smile drifted onto his face. "Now that's what I like to hear."

FIVE

Even though the lights had dimmed to announce the beginning of the stage show, Kieffer still managed to flip a card off the deck and toss it in front of each of the three players sitting around his table. Each of the cards landed in a neat little pile in front of Garrett, Clint and a fourth man who'd joined the game at the last minute. Kieffer set the rest of the deck in front of himself, making sure all of the edges of the cards lined up perfectly and none were disturbing the perfectly smooth stack he'd created.

It took a moment for Clint to realize that the game had even started, since most of his attention was diverted to the showgirls forming a line of wild hair and kicking legs amid a flurry of piano music. They were all beautiful women, but as soon as Alison took her position toward the middle of the line, she easily overshadowed the rest.

The piano players went into a lively rendition of "Camptown Races," which had never sounded better as when it was accompanied by the raucous voices of a dozen women who kicked up their skirts to every fifth note or so. The song was almost half over by the time Alison looked in Clint's direction and gave him a broad smile. She then maneuvered to the edge of the stage and leaned forward to display her generous cleavage, which was highlighted by the plunging neckline of her dress. When she turned her back to him, she spun with enough force to bring her skirts up just high enough so that Clint could see a fleeting glimpse of the tops of her stockings as well as her plump, bare buttocks.

At that moment, he knew what the bartender had meant when he'd said that Alison was one of the more popular girls in the place.

"Are you here to play cards or watch the scenery?"

Clint looked up and saw that it had been Kieffer who'd asked that question. The older man stared at him like a schoolteacher regarding a boy he'd caught staring out the window during his lesson.

Shaking his head, Clint picked up his cards and tossed his ante into the middle of the table. "Sorry, but that's some pretty impressive scenery."

Garrett put his cards down and turned in his seat to look toward the stage. He turned back around with a knowing smile on his face. "That's why I picked this seat right here. Otherwise, I might be likely to forget my own name."

Kieffer didn't so much as crack a smile. "What's your bet, Pat?"

Garrett tossed in a five-dollar chip to pacify the dealer and then took a moment to fully examine his hand.

Since he was next in line, Clint did his best to block out Alison's exotic attempts to reclaim his attention and focused in on his cards. He had a pair of aces, a six of clubs, the five of diamonds and the seven of clubs. "Make it an even ten," he said while throwing the chips into the pot.

The fourth man in the game hadn't even had enough time to introduce himself and, after glancing over to the stern visage the dealer was showing to him, he fanned his cards and took a deep, nervous breath. "I guess I'll stay in for that much."

And the game was on.

Clint did his level best to keep one eye on the show and the other on his game. Normally when he gambled, his attention stayed infallibly on the bets being made, the number of cards being discarded and the possible tells being given off by the other players. But with the dim lighting mixed with the intoxicating glimpses Alison was showing him, it was not an easy chore to keep up with the game.

Perhaps that was why a lot of professional gamblers preferred the Split Hitch. Darker places made it easier to pull off shadowy plays and harder to spot sleight of hand tricks such as palming cards or dealing off the bottom. But as long as the stakes didn't get too high, Clint was satisfied with relaxing and watching the show. Besides, he couldn't help but be more than a little curious as to what other articles of clothing Alison wasn't wearing.

After a few more hands were dealt, the girls took their final bow. Clint was glad he'd been watching at that moment, because Alison made sure to face him as she bent low at the waist, and even from where he was sitting, Clint could see the dark, quarter-sized circles of her nipples peeking out over the top of her dress. With one last wave and flourish of satin and lace, the girls turned and pranced backstage as light flooded into the rest of the saloon.

"Is everyone ready to play now?" Kieffer scolded.

Apparently, Clint wasn't the only one with his eyes diverted from the game. The man sitting to his left and even Garrett himself were staring at the retreating backs of the showgirls as they made their way off stage. As the lights were finally restored to their regular glow, the three men looked at each other and then back to Kieffer, who still sat waiting for a response.

"Get the stick out of yer ass, Kieffer," Garrett said. "Or did you lose something in the war that you forgot to tell me about?"

The older man huffed a few times to show just how far out of whack his nose had been pushed and reached across for the stack of cards. He grumbled a few things under his breath, but was out of stream by the time he dealt the cards. Clint held back his laughter just long enough for the urge to subside.

Up until that moment, Garrett's face had been a stony mask. But as Kieffer threw out the cards one by one, the retired lawman's facade cracked, giving Clint a glimpse of the younger man residing beneath it. The breaks in the stone were repaired, however, as soon as Garrett looked down at his cards. Once the poker face came on, there was no trace of anything vaguely human.

Clint could respect that. He'd heard plenty about Pat Garrett and not a lot of it was very nice. Being the target of quite a few rumors himself, however, Clint knew to take everything he'd heard with a grain of salt. Now that he'd spent some time with the man, Clint was forming an opinion of his own. It would take time, however, for him to see if any of his conclusions panned out.

"I'm out," the man next to Clint grunted as he spitefully pitched his cards onto the table. "Would you fellas mind keepin' an eye on my chips while I run outside to tend to some personal business?"

Garrett shrugged. "If you gotta go, you gotta go."

Kieffer was too busy contemplating his next move to notice.

Clint watched from the corner of his eye as the man pushed away from the table and headed for a small back door behind the bar. After the man was out of sight, Clint turned to Pat and asked, "Does anybody know who that is?"

"Name's Carter," Garrett replied. "He comes in every now and then to play cards. Not very good at it."

Huffing as he laid down his bet, Kieffer put on a smirk that was anything but friendly. "That's an understatement. The man got fleeced just a few days ago. Why do you think he only plays with groups he can trust?"

Clint couldn't resist. "Oh, like fine, upstanding citizens such as yourself?"

"Why yes," Kieffer stated, completely missing the sarcasm in Clint's voice. "And known lawmen like Pat, here."

"You mean *ex*-lawmen." It was Garrett himself who pointed out that fact.

Kieffer dismissed the statement as if he was swatting a fly. "Mister Carter seems to think that as long as he can't be cheated, he can't lose his money."

Clint took one look at the pathetic stack of chips in front of the empty chair and grinned. "I think he needs to come up with another theory."

Nodding, Garrett counted out enough chips to meet Kieffer's bet and then tossed in a few more. "Raise by five dollars."

Clint's hand was only one spade short of a flush. Something in the back of his head told him that he had enough good luck to last a while, so he glanced around the table before moving any chips.

With Carter gone for the moment, Kieffer was the easiest man to read at the table. It had only taken one hand for Clint to notice the subtle shifts in the older man's face that mirrored the emotions he felt when glancing at his cards. Even when they'd been playing in the dark, Clint could see the way his face became a little more pinched when he was disappointed. Conversely, a few of the lines on his forehead would disappear whenever he got the cards he'd wanted.

At the moment, Kieffer couldn't have looked more pinched if he was being squeezed beneath a giant thumb.

Just as Clint was about to push the bet up a little, there came the sharp crack of a gunshot, followed by the shouting of several dozen people.

"So much for that good luck of mine," Clint grumbled as he turned to see what the hell was going on.

SIX

Clint got up from his chair and turned around almost fast enough to overturn the table. The first thing he saw was a thin cloud of smoke hanging over the heads of the crowd, which moved like a stampede to get away from the end of the bar. Shoving his way through the waves of humanity, Clint was bounced off of one body and into another until he'd made it close enough to see what had been the start of it all.

Standing with his back to Clint was a man wearing a battered leather vest and faded jeans. He had a double rig slung around his waist and held one of those guns in his right hand, pointing down toward a body that lay prone on the floor.

"Go ahead and try to get up!" the gunman shouted. "I'll make sure it's the last thing you ever do!"

Even as Clint tried to throw himself at the ranting figure, he was deflected by one of the fleeing bystanders who ran in front of him at the last possible second. Rather than slam into the gunman's back like he'd intended, Clint wound up burying his shoulder into the chest of one of the saloon's dealers who been trying to get behind the bar.

Although he didn't come near the gunman, Clint was able to distract the armed man right before he pulled his trigger a second time. Clint twisted his body as he fell forward, desperately trying to keep the gunman in sight so he could be ready when the man turned his gun toward him.

The dealer hit the ground first, landing in a heap of flailing arms and legs, grunting heavily as Clint knocked all the air from his lungs by falling squarely on top of his body.

Another shot echoed through the saloon, but this time it didn't come from the man Clint was watching. Instead, it came from somewhere closer to Kieffer's poker table, which set off yet another wave of thundering footsteps.

Clint's world shook and rattled around him. His ears rang from the gunshots and his heart thumped brutally inside his rib cage. Fighting through the adrenaline that coursed through his veins, he pushed off the floor with one hand, tossing his body back so that it lay completely on top of the poor, squashed dealer.

All Clint could see was the gunman turning around, tracking Clint's movements with wild, staring eyes. The gun in his hand moved toward Clint's chest, but went off half a second too early, sending another bullet into a piece of floor that Clint had just managed to vacate.

The bullet pounded through the floorboards, sending up a stinging shower of wooden slivers that chewed into the backs of Clint's hands like a swarm of enraged insects. Knowing that he wouldn't be able to dodge another round, Clint continued to roll over the dealer until he landed behind the frightened kid. With one hand on the dealer's belt, Clint used every bit of strength he could dredge up to toss the dealer to one side where he landed in a heap within the mass of escaping customers.

Once he had a clear line of sight, Clint could finally make out what was going on. As for why it was happening . . . well, that would have to be sorted out later.

The gunman's face twisted into a contorted mask of rage. He bared his teeth like an animal as he cocked back the hammer of his gun and twisted his body to get a better shot at Clint. His feet shifted slightly beneath him, which was just enough for the toe of one of his boots to snag on the body laying on the floor, causing the shooter to stumble just as he pulled his trigger.

Clint got up on one knee and went for the Colt at his side.

Without taking his eyes from the gunman in front of him, Clint
snatched the pistol from his holster and brought it up as though
he was merely pointing his finger at the other man. By the time
the gun was aimed, his finger was already squeezing the trigger.

The gunman's wild shot whipped past Clint's head and
smacked into the bar at the precise moment the hammer of
Clint's Colt fell onto its chambered round. The custom-made
pistol bucked once in Clint's hand, belching out a small cloud
of smoke and sparks, spitting its lead through the air.

The gunman jerked back, his face registering more surprise
than pain. For a second, he looked as though he was about to
fire again, but somehow couldn't summon up the strength to
lift his arm. His hand fell to his side and his knees buckled
beneath the rest of his body, dropping him to the floor with a
solid *thump*.

Clint took that moment to get to his feet, keeping his gun
pointed at the wounded man just in case he tried any last-
minute attacks. But no matter how much the gunman wanted
to fire again, all of his energy was flowing from his chest in a
dark crimson stain that spread across the front of his shirt.

Slamming the top of his boot into the gunman's wrist, Clint
sent the other man's gun flying to the ground and well out of
his reach. He then looked down at the first body, which lay on
its belly in an awkward pose with arms and legs bent unnaturally beneath the rest of the torso. Not so much as a twitch
went through the victim's muscles, telling Clint that whoever
that person was, he was as dead as the floorboards he'd fallen
on.

Clint bent down and jammed his gun into the killer's face.
"Who's the man you shot?" he asked, pointing to the body.
"Tell me! What's going on here?"

The killer's breath came in haggard wheezes, followed up
by the wet sucking sound of air struggling to push its way out
through the hole in his chest. He pulled in one last mouthful
of air, held it . . . and went limp in Clint's grasp.

Dropping the killer's body next to the corpse of his victim,
Clint worked his way through the thinning crowd until he could
see where the second volley of gunfire had come from. Judging
by the way Garrett was crouching behind an overturned table

with his own gun drawn, it was safe to say that someone had taken a shot at the ex-lawman as well.

Clint worked his way over to Garrett's side, waiting for the next shot to be fired. He made it to the makeshift barricade without hearing so much as a hint of more gunfire. Once he had his back pressed up against the thick wooden table, Clint looked around. "Where's Kieffer?" he asked. "And the other guy. What happened?"

"Hell if I know," Garrett responded. "Soon as you took off, Kieffer got up to fetch the sheriff and then someone took a shot at him. He must've gotten lost in the stampede that was headed for the door."

"Are you sure whoever shot at you is still—"

Clint's question was cut off and answered by the same shot that came from the other side of the table to punch a hole less than an inch away from his face. Neither man flinched when the bullet passed between them.

Instead, Garrett took a quick glance around the table and pulled himself back around. "Whoever it is, they're next to the stage."

"Just one of them?" Clint asked.

"Hard to say, but I know one way to find out." Garrett raised his gun, cocked back the hammer and crouched like a snake about to strike.

Since a charge was a hell of a lot better than hiding behind something that couldn't even stop a bullet, Clint nodded to Garrett and got ready to make his break from cover.

SEVEN

If it had been anyone else standing in the cramped space where the curtains gathered at the edge of the stage, when pulled back that person would have been spotted like a rake in a haystack. But since the man hiding there was William Krow, all that could be seen of him was a slight bulge in the lump of fabric gathered at the far end of the stage.

Krow pulled his body in with the rest of the material after taking his shot at the overturned poker table. Although the hiding space was ideal for his body type, it made the lanky gunman feel as though he was in a coffin that had been propped up against the wall. The thick folds of musty velvet smothering him from all sides didn't help any as a wave of panic began lapping at Krow's heels.

This hadn't been part of the plan. In fact, he wasn't even supposed to have drawn his gun. Unfortunately, after he'd arranged for the first shooting, he was spotted by Pat Garrett and knew he had to take actions to defend himself.

On top of everything else, he couldn't see a damn thing once he'd pulled himself into cover. With his head wedged inside the thick curtains, the only thing he could hear was the flow of blood racing through his own veins and the thump of his heart, which pumped it.

He stuck his head out and felt the welcome rush of air wash over his face. As soon as his hand popped free, he raised it and thumbed back the hammer of his pistol, eyeing the overturned table not twenty feet away.

Just as he was about to pull his trigger, Krow saw a burst of motion as two figures darted out from behind the table, each heading in opposite directions with their heads held low. Since Krow couldn't make out either of the men's faces in the second he had to pick his target, he simply drew a bead on the one closest to him and took his shot.

The moment Clint dashed away from the table, every one of his senses told him to get ready for the next round of gunfire. Whenever lead started to fly, any sane person's brain told him to run for cover and not come out. But for people who spent a big chunk of their lives on the wrong end of incoming bullets, they had to learn to push that sanity aside and charge into the fray. That was the only way they could stand and fight.

Clint's feet pounded on the floorboards, taking him in the direction of the stage. Instantly, his mind screamed out for him to duck, move, lay down, anything just so long as he got out of the way.

He decided in an instant to trust that voice of caution in the back of his mind, not worrying about where it had come from or why it was so strong. All he knew was that he had to duck, which was exactly what he did . . . less than half a second before the next shot blasted through the air and tore over his head like a bloodthirsty wasp.

Having ducked down low and thrown himself to the side, Clint decided to wait until his footing was steady before squeezing off a shot. Hanging like a ghostly vision in the back of his mind, Clint saw the afterimage of what he'd been looking at only a split second ago.

What he saw was a spot at the edge of the stage where the curtains were drawn and collected in a kind of closet that reached all the way up to the ceiling. Leaning out from those bundled curtains was a skinny man holding a gun. The little bit of memory flickered in Clint's mind and was gone an instant later, its job completed.

Clint blinked once to focus his vision and raised his gun to aim at that part of the stage where he'd seen that fleeting glimpse of the shooter. Trusting his memory, he aimed low and fired.

The bullet punched through the curtains, leaving a puff of dust to mark where the lead had impacted on velvet. At first, Clint thought he'd just let his imagination get carried away after seeing the light glint off of a hook or button or something. When the curtains fluttered and then spit out a scrawny, scarecrow of a man, he thanked whatever part of his brain had been paying attention to that one detail that had tipped him off.

Before Clint could get over to the fallen man, Garrett was already rushing toward the edge of the stage. The former lawman was still swift on his feet and had his gun pressed into the back of the skinny gunman's head before the other man even realized he was on the floor.

"Keep still," Garrett said while kicking away the man's gun. "Or I'll make sure your next stop is a hole in the ground."

The gunman took a second to consider his options. Realizing he had none, he then shifted so that he was laying on his stomach and put his hands behind his head.

Clint scanned the rest of the saloon. The place looked huge since all the other customers had cleared out. There wasn't a lot of places for anyone else to hide, but Clint was not in the mood to leave anything to chance. Making sure to keep his back to the closest wall, Clint moved over to Garrett and said, "You got that one all right?"

"I'd say you were the one that got him, but yeah. I should be fine. It looks to me like he's no stranger to being under arrest."

"You can't arrest nobody, Patsy."

Clint spun around toward the bar, which was where that voice had come from. Standing behind the bar and staring down the barrel of a rifle, was a squat troll in man's clothes with an upper lip covered in thick, bushy hair. His voice had a slight accent, but nothing Clint could immediately recognize.

"What are you doing here, Drezdev?" Garrett asked. "I thought I told you I didn't want to see you around here any more."

"You got no badge, which means nobody has to listen to a damn thing that comes out of that mouth of yours. And shooting you ain't no big thing either. Not so long as it was a fair fight."

Clint's hand flickered in one quick motion, bringing his Colt around to point at Drezdev. "Murder is murder," he said. "And I don't take kindly to murderers."

EIGHT

Drezdev's upper body twisted slowly until he was pointing the rifle directly at Clint's face. Although Clint wasn't sure if the ugly little man could hit anything from this distance, he wasn't about to give him a chance to prove himself. Instinctively, Clint's muscles tensed and his eyes flicked from side to side, looking for the best place to jump if he thought the rifle was going to go off.

Garrett straightened up to his full height. Now that he wasn't sitting at the table or crouching behind it, Garrett showed just how tall he truly was. Although he was by no means a giant, he held himself with the strength and confidence of a man used to wearing a badge. Even when he didn't have the power of the law behind him, he still wore that power in his face and posture.

"What the hell is all this about?" Garrett asked.

Just then, another man rose up from behind the opposite end of the bar as Drezdev. He stood about the same height as the man with the rifle, but carried more of his weight in the thick muscles that covered his body like armor plates.

"This is about business, Pat," Carlyle said. "Something you wouldn't know a whole lot about."

Garrett held his gun aimed at Drezdev, but shifted it between the two men standing behind the bar. Finally, he straightened his arm and aimed at a spot in between them where he could be ready to take a shot at either one. "If you're going to shoot, then do it. Otherwise, I'll just take the first shot myself."

Shaking his head, Drezdev shrugged and looked toward Clint. "No need for that. We're just about done here, anyways."

"Who's the man your partner killed?" Clint asked.

Drezdev acted as though he was confused by the question. The effort made him look like a child who was very bad at lying. He rolled his eyes and rubbed his chin dramatically. "Partner? Oh, you mean that one there?" he said, pointing toward the floor where the two bodies lay. "Didn't you get a good look at him?"

Clint thought back to when he'd shot the first gunman and still he couldn't quite make out the face of that man that had been lying on the floor. However, thinking back to the clothes the man had been wearing, Clint had a pretty good idea who it was. "Carter?" he asked.

Drezdev nodded. "That's right. And it was an awful shame for you and Pat to kill him like that over something like a couple bad hands of cards."

Garrett's face twisted with obvious confusion, mirroring the same thing that was running through Clint's mind. "You must be drunk," Garrett said. "Because you're not making a bit of sense."

"I got witnesses who saw your friend Adams shoot Carter and this other one laying beside him. They tell me you even helped and shot poor Krow over there." When Drezdev pointed toward Krow, the skinny man struggled to get to his feet, but only made it a few steps before dropping back to the ground, clutching the wound in his lower ribs.

Clint looked over to Garrett, searching for a way through the haze that had just settled over the conversation. "Could somebody tell me what the hell he's talking about? By the time I got over there, Carter was already dead."

"It doesn't matter, Adams," Garrett said. "At least not right now."

"Why? Who's going to believe him?"

Pointing to the front door, Garrett holstered his weapon and said, "They are."

Clint looked to where Garrett was pointing and saw a group of four men storm into the saloon with guns drawn. They fanned out as soon as they got inside, to form a small firing line. Standing in the middle of that line was an older man wearing a battered duster and a well-worn Stetson on top of his head. Pinned to his chest was a tin star that glimmered in the reflected lantern light.

"Don't anybody move," the sheriff warned.

Drezdev smiled smugly at Clint and Garrett as he tossed down his rifle and held up his hands. "They shot three men, sheriff. Including two of 'em that were my friends."

"Th—that's right," Krow grunted as he bit back a wave of pain that flooded from his open wound. Pointing at Clint with a hand drenched in his own blood, he grunted, "That one nearly killed me. Look what he done!"

Although the sheriff's deputies were nothing but scared young men, they were still scared *armed* young men and they all turned to point their guns at Clint. The sheriff stepped forward and held out his hand. "I need to ask for your gun, mister."

Clint looked first at Garrett, who only shrugged back at him.

"Sorry, Adams," Garrett said. "But I'm not in the habit of firing on the law."

"I know," Clint replied. "Neither am I."

Stuck in a tighter spot than the one Krow had been using, Clint spun his Colt so he could place the handle into the sheriff's hand . . . and surrendered.

NINE

Of all the places Clint thought he would wind up at the end of the night, the White Sands jail was most definitely not one of them.

He'd seen the process plenty of times. As soon as the law showed up, the accused would start talking away about how they were innocent and being treated unfairly while the sheriff did his level best to ignore every word and just keep control of his prisoner. By the time he was being led down the street by a deputy holding either one of his arms, Clint realized that he was now in the role of prisoner and was playing it right to the hilt. Endless accusations and all.

"This is a big mistake," he said for the tenth time to the back of the sheriff's head. "I was only trying to help in there and those men back there were the ones shooting at me. Why not take them in as well?"

"Because," the sheriff said impatiently, "I know where to find those men whenever I need to and right now, I don't have any reason to bring them in. Besides, they weren't the only ones who say you started this whole mess."

"What?" Clint said as his anger flared and he tried to think of anyone in that saloon that might have seen something that could be used against him. His anger flared even more when he realized that he hadn't done anything wrong at all. The more he thought about it, the more the whole situation just plain stank. "Who saw what? There wasn't even anything to see."

The sheriff, who'd been marching in front of the rest as though he wasn't even a part of the small caravan, stopped in his tracks and slowly turned around. "Look, I don't know what the hell happened in that saloon. All I got to go on is what I was told. If we find that you were in the right, you'll go free. But until then, the only one with any fingers being pointed at him is you. Now are you going to cooperate or is this gonna have to be done the hard way?"

Clint took a breath and let it out. Even though he was mad enough to just break away from the deputies and head off on his own, he knew the lawmen were only doing their jobs. Doing anything but what they wanted at this point would only make things worse for everybody. "Fine," he grumbled. "When's my court date?"

"You can see Judge Fountain in the morning. He's a fair man and will hear you out first thing tomorrow. If it's like you say it was, you won't have a problem."

After allowing himself to be paraded through the street like a criminal and shut inside a cramped steel cage, Clint stood with his back against a cold stone wall and tried to keep his calm. The only furnishings inside the cell was a broken hardwood bench and a pot to piss in. Well, at least he had that much. Amazingly enough, even those two things made the oversized stone closet of a room seem cramped.

So many things ran through Clint's brain. In fact, there was so much going on inside his head that it made him more and more tired every time he thought about it. All of that, combined with everything else that had happened, made even the rickety bench look inviting. Clint sat down and slowly rested his weight on the shaky wooden structure, preparing himself for the moment when the damn thing would just up and break into splinters beneath him.

Surprisingly enough, the bench held. Both man and bench shifted a few times and then groaned and creaked a bit before settling in. Once Clint was finally sitting with one shoulder on and the other off the bench, his head propped up against the wall and one foot hanging out between the steel bars, he actually started to feel himself calm down.

Despite the situation and his accommodations, Clint had to laugh. He shook his head, closed his eyes and took comfort that he was doing the only thing he could possibly do at this moment.

Wait.

TEN

Drezdev stood outside the Split Hitch, staring into the petrified face of one of the dealers. "You talked to the sheriff?"

The dealer, who shook like a leaf when he felt the steel barrel of Drezdev's pistol nudging against his stomach, nodded quickly and tried to back away. Having already been pushed up against the wall of the saloon, he didn't have very far to go. "Y–yeah. I told him just what you said."

"And what's that?"

Swallowing hard to free up his vocal chords, the dealer looked as though he was about to pass out from the combined effort of standing up and talking to Drezdev. "All I said was that I saw that man—the one sitting with Mister Garrett—I saw him shoot Mister Carter."

"And?" Drezdev pressed while jabbing his pistol a little deeper into the dealer's gut.

"A-and that he shot them other two."

Drezdev seemed to peer into the dealer's soul with eyes that burned with a seething fire. He held his gaze a little longer just to put the scare into the quivering figure at the other end of his gun before finally pulling his pistol away. "Good. Now you be sure to remember what you said, 'cause if you say anything different to anyone else, I'll come back for ya."

The instant Drezdev backed off a few steps, the dealer was off and running. He dashed down the alley toward the front of the saloon and kept right on going until even his footsteps faded away. When he was gone, another figure emerged from the nearby shadows and came up next to Drezdev.

Carlyle's squat, muscular frame looked like another chunk of the wall to the next building in the murky darkness. He'd let his long, black hair flow freely, which gave him the appearance of wearing a chunk of the night wrapped around his shoulders. He turned and watched the dealer flee, wearing a grim smile on his face. "You never miss a chance to do that, do you?"

"What?" Drezdev asked without looking at the other man.

"Put the fear of God into somebody. I swear if you thought it would work on me, you'd be trying that shit right now."

Wheeling around, Drezdev raised his pistol and rammed it up beneath Carlyle's ribs. "Every man's scared of something," he snarled. "And if you're a smart man, you're scared of me."

Carlyle's expression was completely blank. For the next few seconds, both men simply stared at each other, waiting for the other to blink. At once, both of them started laughing. The sound was far from a joyous one, resembling something closer to the rumble of an approaching storm. Drezdev holstered his gun and Carlyle took his hand away from the other man's stomach.

It was just then that Drezdev looked down and realized that Carlyle had gotten the blade of his hunting knife right up against his belly. "You still got the old touch," Drezdev said with a hint of true respect. Carlyle slid the knife back into it scabbard. "But you never could get the drop on me. Did you find out what happened to Krow?"

"The bullet took a bite out of him just below the ribs. It passed through the meat, though, so I got him to the doc and he's patched up. Should be on his feet again soon. What about that boy of yours?"

"Who're you talking about?"

"The one you paid to shoot Carter."

"Oh, that one." Drezdev gave a dismissive snort and spat on the ground. "I told him he'd have a spot with us if he did that one job good enough. Adams made sure I didn't have to put up with that one's company for very long."

"Did he really have a chance?"

Nodding, Drezdev said, "Sure he did. But if Adams hadn't put him down, I would've taken him out after the sheriff cleared out."

"So what's next?"

"Next, we take advantage of the time we gave ourselves by making sure that Adams and Garrett are too busy to notice the rest of what we got going on."

"Garrett didn't wind up in a cell," Carlyle pointed out. "He might not even care what happened to Adams."

· "No, but he was there and saw what happened. He'll make it his business to talk to the sheriff. And that will keep another problem out of our hair for a little while. With Adams in the cage we'll be able to do our job and get out of town before anyone knows we're gone."

"Speaking of our job, maybe we should get started while we can."

"No need for hurrying," Drezdev said as he turned and started leisurely walking down the alley. "We got all the time in the world."

They walked out to the front of the saloon and tipped their hats to the deputy who had been left posted outside the door. Ignoring the cautious stares from the lawman, Drezdev and Carlyle strolled down the street as though they didn't have a care in the world.

"By the way," Carlyle said. "I thought Carter had another week to pay back them gambling debts he owned before you were coming after him."

Drezdev looked up at the stars and shrugged. "Changed my mind. I also wanted to send a message. Just a little notice to you and Krow."

"Is that so?"

"Yep," Drezdev said as he turned his eyes from the stars and looked straight at Carlyle. "Carter tried my patience and thought he could get away with something. He was wrong."

"What's the matter? You don't trust us?"

"I don't trust nobody. You two just do yer parts and we'll

all walk away happy. You cross me and I'll bury you just the same as I did Carter."

Carlyle was far from impressed with Carter's death. He'd seen more men die than he could even remember. What made him think was the way Drezdev had gone about the shooting. Carlyle had never seen the gunman before in his life until the other man stepped out of a crowd and put a bullet into Mr. Carter. That, more than anything else, was the real message Drezdev was trying to send.

Death could come from anyone and anywhere.

Living outside the law for as long as Carlyle and the others had, they'd all learned that lesson pretty well. But there had always been a code. There had always been an understanding that the normal ruthlessness didn't apply to one another. They would risk life and limb for each other while letting the rest of the world go to hell. Protect the few and steal from the rest. That had been the cardinal rule of the lawless.

As of this moment, Drezdev had made it clear that he now set himself above those rules and he wanted to make sure that everyone knew it.

"That's fine with me," Carlyle said, holding his hands up as though he was the one being robbed. "Have it any way you like it. I ain't about to pass up a sweet deal like this job."

Drezdev stood with his feet planted and his back straightened as much as his crooked spine would allow. "And I'm the leader now, right? No more questions and no more debate. I lead this gang and we do what I say."

Thinking about what he'd just learned, Carlyle nodded and smiled sheepishly, "You made your point and we'll stick to it. Any way you want to go."

ELEVEN

Clint awoke to a sharp, blinding pain in his ankle. At first, the thing that surprised him the most was the fact that he'd been able to fall asleep at all with every joint and muscle in his body crying out for mercy. He tried to sit up and felt his bones rubbing against the unforgiving hardwood bench that was the closest thing to a bed his cell had to offer.

Suddenly, everything came rushing back at him through the thick haze of sleep that had clubbed him over the head despite his body's protests. He was still in White Sands. Still in jail. Still in a mess of trouble.

The next thing to come as a surprise was the sight of who was standing on the other side of his bars, looking down at him with an amused smile on her face.

Still dressed in the black and red dress that she'd worn in the Split Hitch Saloon earlier that evening, Alison shook her head slowly as though she was taking in a stage show herself. Next to her was one of the sheriff's deputies who fumbled with the key inside the cell door's lock, twisting and cranking the metal shard with every muscle in his arm.

"You don't really want to talk to him right now, do you?" the deputy asked hopefully.

"Sorry, Dave," she said while giving the younger man a

43

quick look. "But I need to see him right this instant."

That one, quick look was more than enough to make the deputy forget about the other complaints he'd had prepared and ready to go. In fact, it even made him twist the key a little harder, causing the old mechanism to snap into place and sending a piece of the bars swinging out in his direction.

The pain in Clint's ankle stabbed through his entire leg one more time. He pulled his foot back from the bars less than half a second before the bottom part of his leg was torn off and pulled away from his body with the rest of the door. Shifting down on his bench to make sure he had enough slack to maneuver his foot, Clint wound up with his back flat against the hardwood and his head thumping against one of the broken arm rests. One foot was touching the floor while the other lay propped up against the bars, leaving his legs in an extraordinarily uncomfortable Y position as Alison came strolling inside the cell.

"Not exactly the way I expected to find you," she said.

The deputy stood in the doorway with his hands resting on his hips, nervously shifting his eyes between Alison and Clint. "You sure about this, ma'am?"

"Yes, Dave. It's all right." Turning to give the deputy a lingering look with her wide brown eyes, she asked, "You'll be right outside, won't you?"

"Actually, I should probably stay here so—"

"I wouldn't want to bother you. Mister Adams and I are old friends. You can just leave me in here and I'll call you when I'm ready to go. After all, I wouldn't want to be a nuisance and trouble you any more than I already have."

The deputy shook his head warily. "Sorry, ma'am. I just can't let you in there any longer. Just give him the bag and I'll let you talk all you want through the bars like every other visitor."

Pouting with her lower lip extended in a strangely exotic way, Alison handed over a small cloth sack that Clint hadn't seen before. At the last second, the deputy gently took it from her hand, opened it and rooted through carefully.

"Just making sure," the lawman said before tossing it onto Clint's bench. He then took hold of Alison's arm and pulled her back a few steps so that he could shut and lock the cell door. "I'll be at the end of the hall so if—"

"Can't I talk to him alone?" she asked with her lips turned down in that little pout.

"I've got to be here."

"Then," she said while holding her hands over her head and cocking her hip to one side. "Why don't you search me? Just to make sure."

The deputy stepped up to her and started to turn away again. Alison took his hands in hers and guided them over her body. Keeping her eyes locked on his, she guided the deputy's palms down her sides, over her hips, around to her buttocks and then back up until they came to a rest on her firm, rounded breasts. For a second, the young man looked as though he was about to break into a sweat. Then, his hands closed around her and she took in a quick gasp of air.

"You do that so well," she whispered.

After keeping his hands on her for a few more seconds, the deputy peeled them off her body and forced himself to take a few steps back. "Ten minutes," the deputy said to her. "That's all you get before I come back to fetch you. He tries anything, you just holler."

Alison stood with her head bowed and her hands clasped in front of her. "I sure will, Dave. Thank you."

The deputy was unable to keep the smile off his face. After taking one last look at Clint, he turned and headed back down the small hallway that led to the main room of the sheriff's office. The door *thumped* shut behind him and the lock slid into place with a rusted screech.

"I brought that for you," Alison said once the sounds stopped echoing in the barren stretch of cells.

There were only two other cells besides Clint's and, at the moment, his was the only one occupied.

Clint opened the small sack she'd given him and looked inside. It contained a few sandwiches, an apple and what turned out to be a piece of blackberry pie wrapped in a napkin. It smelled delicious and it took every bit of Clint's self-control not to shove it in his mouth and swallow it down like a ravenous animal.

Alison shifted on her feet, running her hands up and down the cold iron bars. "I figured they'd be giving you your meal right about now and thought you might prefer something a little more . . . edible."

Taking out one of the sandwiches, Clint opened it and saw a few slices of beef in between the soft white bread. "Why are you doing this?" he asked.

"I don't know if you remember, but I was at the Split Hitch last night."

"Oh, I remember you."

Smiling, she looked down at the floor and then back up at Clint. Although the demure display didn't suit her, the dancer somehow managed to pull it off. "I heard Mick and Tom talking about you. They know who you are, Mister Adams. They said they wanted to get you out of the way and were pretty sure that Judge Fountain will keep you here for a good long while."

"That's not surprising, considering they got a bunch of hand-picked witnesses who somehow all managed to swear that I was the only one shooting at anyone back there." He took a bite of the sandwich and closed his eyes to savor the way the cuts of meat melted in his mouth. The bread was thick and just a little sweet, even after soaking up the faint taste of cooking fires.

When he started talking again, the first sandwich was gone. Alison watched him with interest, leaning against the bars. "But why did you come down here?" he asked. "You told the deputy we went way back, but I don't recall—"

"We've never met before. But I do know who you are. You're the Gunsmith. I've seen plenty of gunfighters come through here. Wyatt Earp, Doc Holliday, even William Bonney stopped by one time a few years back. Every one of them moved like . . . cats." Now, her body had started slowly moving back and forth as her hands stroked the bars tenderly up and down. "They were like tigers," she said, her eyes growing wider. "But none of them were like you."

Alison fixed her eyes on Clint as though she was trying to get him to walk through the bars. Her mouth opened slightly and the tip of her tongue slipped out to slowly lick her plump, red upper lip. "I wanted to meet you. Get closer to you. Actually, I was hoping to get the deputy to let me in there with you so I could see what it was like to feel your muscles move and touch your body . . ."

Her words trailed off, but her eyes never strayed from Clint. Looking him over, she seemed to be every bit as hungry as he was, breathing heavily so that her supple breasts heaved beneath the confines of her black and red dress. "I came over here as soon as I could. Do you think I'm too forward?"

Clint took the second sandwich with him as he got up and stepped up close to the bars. Leaning against the wall, he took his time examining the way she stood. Alison's hands drifted from the bars to push a few strands of hair away from her face. After moving her dark brown locks behind one ear, she trailed her fingers down the side of her neck and along the plunging neckline of her dress. After a full night's worth of dancing, her skin was flushed and glistening with a fine layer of sweat. She smelled sweet and musky. Her skin looked smoother than cream.

"I don't think 'forward' is quite enough to describe you," Clint said. "But don't get me wrong. I appreciate the meal."

"Good," she said as she slipped her hand into her dress pocket. "Because I know you'll love dessert."

Clint nearly spit out the bite of sandwich he'd taken when he saw what was in Alison's hand. Fit snugly between her fingers was an old metal key which, in turn, fit perfectly into the lock on Clint's cell door.

"What the hell are you doing?" he asked. "If you think I'm breaking out of here, you've got another thing coming."

"You're not going anywhere," she said as she swung the door open and stepped inside. "I promised Dave that much back at the saloon when I knew you were being held here. He knows I won't try nothing illegal with you." She pulled the door shut behind her and pressed her body up against Clint's. "Just like he knows to give us a little more than ten minutes together."

TWELVE

Despite every reasonable bone in his body, Clint couldn't help but be intrigued by the way Alison had gone about meeting up with him. At first, he'd thought that she'd confused him for someone more along the lines of the outlaws she'd met before. But as soon as she closed the cell door behind herself, Alison tossed the key onto his bench and began running her hands up and down his chest.

"You've probably met a lot of women like me, haven't you, Clint?" Sliding her hands up underneath his shirt, Alison raked her fingernails along Clint's skin just hard enough to send an erotic chill through his body.

"No," Clint said in a hoarse whisper. "I can safely say that I haven't run into many women like you."

She smiled as her eyes narrowed, raw passion taking over her face and body. "I've never done anything like this before, but when I saw you . . . I couldn't help myself."

"What about the sheriff?" Clint asked as Alison busied herself with pulling open his shirt and peeling it off of his body.

"I've heard plenty about you," she whispered into his ear. "I know you're a good man. And besides, even though I might be able to get the deputy wrapped around my finger doesn't mean I'm ready to break you out of here. All I want is some time alone with you . . . right *now*."

This was crazy.

Clint knew it and so did she, but as their hands began roaming over each other's hips and skin, probing beneath layers of clothing to touch new areas and revel in the pleasure they were giving to one another, neither one cared too much for sanity. All they wanted was to keep feeling what they were feeling, to keep savoring the sensation as it washed over them like a tidal wave.

Clint's shirt dropped to the floor, followed seconds later by Alison's dress, which fell away from her body to land in a soft black-and-red heap around her feet. As she'd made clear enough earlier in the Split Hitch, she was wearing nothing beneath her dress besides a pair of black leather boots, which laced all the way up to her knees.

Alison pressed her lips against Clint's mouth roughly at first, kissing him as though she wanted only to devour him. Her tongue flicked against his lips and then probed deeply to entwine with his as a rumbling moan swelled up from the back of her throat.

All the while, she tugged at his clothing until he stood naked before her. Moving her eyes slowly over his form, she reached down to take hold of his penis with both hands, stroking it until it was fully erect. She pressed her hips against him so that the tip of his cock brushed against the tender folds of skin between her legs. The dampness there allowed him to slide inside easily, which caused Alison to take in a long, deep breath. She let it out while propping one leg up against the wall and began pumping her hips back and forth.

Clint leaned back and watched her body move. Alison's firm, round breasts bounced slightly, her nipples hardening into little pink nubs. As she ground against his body, she leaned her head back and let her hair flow over her shoulder blades while grabbing hold of Clint's hands to keep her from falling.

Unable to hold himself back any longer, Clint reached around and cupped her firm, supple buttocks and lifted her up off of her feet. As soon as he stepped away from the wall, Clint turned in a half circle so that it was her back that was pushed up against the stone. Alison wrapped both legs around his waist and leaned in to nibble on his ear while sliding her fingers through his hair.

Clint could feel the thick muscles in her legs as they clenched around him, pulling him in closer as her hips strained and bucked against him. The slickness between her thighs was hot and luxurious, enveloping him as his cock burrowed deep inside of her body. When he began pumping with a strong, steady rhythm, Clint could hear Alison grunting with pleasure in his ear, responding to every single stroke.

Both of his hands were supporting Alison's perfectly rounded backside. Like the rest of her body, it was trim and toned after countless nights spent dancing on stage. Even her stomach was impressively contoured. Clint looked down at the line of her body that started with her chin and ran all the way between her soft breasts, down the smooth slope of her abdomen and ended with the thick patch of downy hair between her legs.

Alison opened her eyes as though she could feel Clint's gaze moving down her body. She relaxed her legs and pressed Clint away with both palms placed flat against his sweating chest. Without saying a word, she walked past him and over to the bench. Slowly, she bent at the waist until her fingertips were resting on the hardwood and her bottom was pushed slightly out toward Clint.

Taking a second or two to admire her from this angle, Clint moved up behind her and ran his hands down along her back and over the perfectly rounded curve of her buttocks. "If I knew it was going to be like this," he said while sliding his fingers inside the wet lips between her thighs, "I would've gotten arrested a long time ago."

Alison looked over her shoulder and smiled before leaning down a bit more and lowering her head so that her dark brown hair cascaded over her face and neck.

Using his fingers to rub up and down her pussy lips, Clint quickened his pace until he could hear Alison's breathing speed up and become more and more labored. When he moved one of his fingertips onto the swollen nub of skin over her opening,

Clint reached out with his other hand to gently massage her breast.

"Don't torture me, Clint," she moaned softly. "Please."

Clint obliged her by sliding his cock inside of her and driving it in as far as he could go. Gripping her backside with both hands, he began pounding into her until she needed to brace herself with both hands on the bench.

Every time his hips met her body, Alison had to strain to keep from crying out as loud as she could. She savored the feel of his rigid penis entering her, the caress of his hands on her skin, the lingering memory of his breath on her neck. The more she thought about how good Clint was making her feel, she began to shudder as those sensations became even more powerful, sending waves of pleasure through her flesh that only became more powerful with every stroke.

Clint reached down and took a handful of Alison's hair, enjoying its silken texture between his fingers. As soon as he did, she leaned her head back and groaned louder. Just then, her entire body began to tremble, the muscles in her vagina tensed and held on tightly to him. When her orgasm grew inside of her and finally exploded, every part of her body responded to intensify the sensation that coursed throughout every muscle and every fiber of her being.

Feeling as though the cell was tilting and spinning around him, Clint grabbed hold of Alison's hair and pulled just hard enough to bring another moan of pleasure from her lips. He pounded into her once more, keeping his shaft buried all the way inside of her as the muscles between her legs tightened and twitched, massaging him until his own climax rocked through his body with so much force that his knees almost buckled beneath him.

They dressed slowly, enjoying the sight of the other's naked body moving so close to one another as they pulled on their clothing piece by piece. Alison gave him one last, lingering kiss before using the key to let herself out. Once she'd shut him back inside, she turned and started walking down the hall.

Clint had plenty of questions he wanted to ask her, but for some reason, he just couldn't find the words before she was gone.

THIRTEEN

After spending an entire night behind the bar at the Split Hitch Saloon, Ben was more than ready to get out from the smoke-filled building and head down the street toward his home. Although it wasn't much more than a room at a boardinghouse in the run-down part of town, it was still home and Ben was going to be so happy to see it.

He walked in the morning light, squinting and raising his hands against the blazing sun, until he came to the corner only half a block away from home. As soon as he made the turn, he headed away from the people who'd been going to and from the restaurants and stores near the Split Hitch and into a stretch of road that was fairly deserted at this time of day.

He was used to the solitude of the area which was, in fact, one of the reasons he'd chosen to live there. Far away from the noises and commotion that filled every one of his working hours, the boardinghouse was in a quiet area that had been shunned by the bigger businesses and richer families. When he got within sight of his building, Ben rubbed at his tired eyes and thought about how good it would feel when his back met the familiar lumps of his mattress.

Suddenly, the sound of footsteps caught his attention. They came at him from two sides, one from behind and the other from his right. Before he could take his hands away from his eyes, he felt a vice-like grip close around his right wrist, pulling his arm down and behind him in a way that sent jagged shards of pain through his entire shoulder.

"What the hell?" he started to say before another set of hands came from behind to clamp over his mouth.

Ben's first instinct was to struggle against whoever was trying to hold him down. He swiveled his body around, trying to wrench his arm free. But the grip on his wrist was too tight and as soon as he stopped moving, the bones in his shoulder crunched together right before the wet snapping sound announced that they'd broken completely.

Although he tried to say something, even call out for help, the pain was too great for Ben to overcome. Any sound he made came out as a strained wheezing, followed by a reflexive grunt. Through the agonizing haze that had clouded his vision, Ben could see the faces of his attackers.

He recognized them from the saloon, but never thought of them as anything besides regular customers. Mick Drezdev fought to move behind him so he could once again press his hand over Ben's mouth. This time, the bartender could feel the wet handkerchief being shoved in as his jaw was forced open. Tom Carlyle was holding onto both of the bartender's wrists by this time, preventing him from going for the old pistol he kept at his side for emergencies just like this one.

"Come on, Ben," Drezdev said while straining to keep from getting thrown off the bartender's back. "Make it easy on yerself."

Fighting through all the pain that was coursing through his upper body, Ben wrenched one arm free and went for his gun. Carlyle responded by sending out a quick, powerful jab to that elbow, which nearly gave Ben another break in his skeleton to worry about.

The two outlaws worked together, one pushing while the other pulled, to get the big man moving toward a nearby door that had been left open by Drezdev. It only took a few seconds to get the bartender inside and out of the middle of the street. Drezdev reached down and snatched the pistol from Ben's belt so he could send the old weapon bouncing off of the bartender's skull.

For a moment, Carlyle thought his partner was going to pull the trigger after he pressed the gun to Ben's head. Drezdev's hand shook with rage, but then he finally caught hold of his temper before Ben's forehead was blown onto the floor.

"Check outside," Drezdev said. "See if anyone saw what happened."

Carlyle peeked out the door and then stepped into the empty street. "I don't see anyone," he said after a few seconds. "Don't hear anyone either."

"Then help me tie up this piece of shit so we can get out of here."

Running on sheer adrenaline and survival instinct, Ben fought through his pain against the outlaws' attempt to tie his hands behind his back. But Carlyle and Drezdev were strong enough to loop their rope around Ben's wrists. Whenever the bartender gave them too much trouble, they simply pulled up on his arms and wrenched the broken bones hard enough to make the consciousness in Ben's eyes dim like a candle in a stiff breeze.

One straight left across Ben's jaw was enough to put that flame out for good. It was enough to put Ben out for a few hours, anyway, and the big man slumped over against the wall as he was pitched headlong into a cold, black sleep.

Before the bartender could even fall to one side, Carlyle was crouching down next to him and rooting through his pockets with both hands. In a matter of seconds, he'd found what he was looking for and stood up clutching a set of small keys on a rusted brass ring.

"Here we go," Carlyle said triumphantly. "We're in business."

"Thank God," Drezdev said. Looking down at the slumbering barkeep, he thrust his boot deep into Ben's gut just for spite. "I thought he was gonna go to his grave over this. He already cost us more time than we should've spent here."

"Let's get him to the barn and then collect the others. After that, we'll head over to the general store and in an hour, we'll be out of this damn town."

Both men took out small watches from their pockets, checked them and then snapped them shut.

Drezdev nodded and said, "Let's do this."

FOURTEEN

The meal that Alison had brought him was still sitting comfortably in Clint's stomach when he heard the door at the end of the jail cells open once again. Several sets of footsteps came down the hall and Clint didn't bother getting up to see who it was since he'd actually managed to find a spot on the bench that didn't put cramps in his back. Rather than lose that minor accomplishment, he sat and waited for his newest visitors to come to him.

The first person he saw was the deputy who'd let Alison in for her extended visit. The younger lawman scanned the area nervously as though he half expected the showgirl to still be lounging around next to the prisoner. Following closely behind him was the sheriff, who was talking to another group of people bringing up the rear.

One of those last men was Pat Garrett. Seeing him in the cramped quarters of the jail, Clint was surprised at how much bigger the ex-lawman looked. Standing well over six feet tall, Garrett towered over the rest with a distinguished, almost regal presence that was only accentuated by his quiet demeanor. Everyone else seemed to be talking to him, waiting for him to say a few words that would steer the rest of the conversation.

The only man in the group who didn't seem to defer to

Garrett was the one who walked at the end of the line. An older man with a full head of silvery gray hair that was kept swept back immaculately from his forehead, this final arrival stepped right past the others until he could peer directly into Clint's cell.

"Is this the accused?" the slender gray-haired figure asked.

The sheriff nodded. "Yessir, Judge Fountain. This is him, alright."

Judge Fountain clasped his hands behind his back and rocked back and forth on his heels a few times. Studying Clint as though he didn't expect the prisoner to be capable of speech, the judge nodded once to himself before turning to Garrett. "You were there, Pat. Tell me what you saw."

Although there was respect in Garrett's voice, there was still strength and resolve left in his words as well. It was obvious that Garrett wasn't vying for favor, which somehow seemed to make Fountain listen even closer to what he had to say. "Just like I told you before, sir. We heard the shots and Mister Adams went to investigate. During that time, he and I both were jumped by Drezdev and his . . . friends. They obviously wanted to kill us, so we fought back the best we could. I didn't see Adams kill anyone, but if he did, I'd say that it was a clear-cut case of self defense."

Turning his eyes back toward Clint, Judge Fountain regarded him with stern consternation. Clint had already gotten to his feet by this time and as he was about to say something on his own behalf, Garrett shook his head just enough to warn Clint off. Going against his better judgment, Clint bit his tongue and leaned against the back wall of his cell.

Finally, Judge Fountain shifted his eyes slightly so that he was looking directly at Clint's face rather than regarding him like a moving piece of the cell wall. "So, Mister Adams, is it? What have you got to say for yourself about this entire affair?"

Clint straightened up and took a few steps forward. Only the deputy took a half-step back while the sheriff, Garrett and Fountain all held their ground. In fact, none of the others even looked concerned that Clint might act inappropriately as he got closer to the bars.

"It sounds to me like Mister Garrett has told you just about all there is," Clint said. "I was in the Split Hitch trying to do nothing besides play some cards and enjoy the show."

Even though Clint was addressing the judge, he couldn't miss the sly look he got from the deputy who was the one person who knew just how much Clint had enjoyed his own private show earlier in his cell.

But everyone else stood formally in front of him as though court was in session.

Focusing on Judge Fountain, Clint went on. "I heard the shot and went over to see if I could help and was faced down by a man who I can only guess was the one who'd done the shooting."

"And he threatened you?" the judge asked.

"Yes, he did. I warned him to back off and put down his gun, but he took a shot at me first and I defended myself by putting a bullet into him. There were more shots and so I went back to help Mister Garrett who was being attacked by at least one other gunman. I shot him, but not to kill. When the law arrived, they spoke to some men who told the sheriff what he wanted the law to hear so that I was taken—"

"To be fair, Mister Adams," Fountain interrupted, "you really can't know everything the sheriff was told. Go on."

Clint kept himself from saying something out of line or arguing with the judge since that would only make himself look worse. "I guess that's it then."

"Are you aware that there were witnesses who state that you were the one who started everything?"

"Yes. I was told that much."

"And what have you to say about that?"

Shrugging, Clint replied, "Nothing that I can prove. All I can figure is that they were too scared to go against the man who started the shooting. That same man might have told them they were next if—"

Judge Fountain held up one hand and shook his head like a disapproving schoolmaster. "I'm not interested in your guesswork or opinions. All I want is the facts."

"Then I guess I've said everything I can say."

Nodding slowly, Judge Fountain's eyes shifted slightly away from Clint. The subtle change was more than enough to let

Clint know that he was being considered a part of the scenery again and shouldn't even bother trying to say anything else unless it was important and backed in solid proof. Although Clint had plenty to say, he didn't have the backing just yet, so he decided to keep his mouth shut and see what happened.

"I've heard enough," Fountain declared. "Sheriff, who were the men who you talked to at the Split Hitch?"

"Mick Drezdev and Tom Carlyle."

"And William Krow was the one injured by Mister Adams?"

"Yessir."

For the first time, the judge's solid demeanor unraveled slightly, revealing a bit of true fatigue beneath his rocky surface. "I've dealt with those men more times than I can count even if I could use another man's fingers and toes. In fact, I spoke to Drezdev and Krow in the cell right next to this one not too long ago, am I correct?"

Looking over to the now-vacant cell next to Clint's, the sheriff smirked a bit and nodded. "Yessir. You sure did."

"I don't want to waste valuable court time on this matter and I sure as hell don't want to listen to another batch of Drezdev's pathetic lies." With a quick swipe of his hand, Judge Fountain nodded to the sheriff and decreed, "I want you to find those witnesses and question them again. Assure them that they'll have the full protection of the law if they're too afraid to tell the truth this time. As soon as someone steps forward, bring in those three and put them back in their cell. I don't care if you have to drag Mister Krow out of the doctor's office to do it, either. They've been enough of a pain in this town's ass to be tolerated any further."

"Excuse me, Judge Fountain." It was the deputy who spoke up this time.

The judge wheeled around and fixed his eyes upon the younger man. "Yes?"

"Actually, someone already has stepped forward."

First the judge looked to Garrett and then the sheriff, both of whom shrugged in response. "Who are you talking about? Why wasn't I told this before?"

"Go on, Dave," the sheriff prodded. "Say your peace."

"One of the girls who dances at the Split Hitch talked to me earlier today," Dave said. "She told me what happened. In fact, it sounded a lot like what Mister Garrett and . . . the prisoner were saying."

Fountain seemed to consider this for about a second and a half before saying, "Fine. I'll remember that when this matter eventually comes to my courtroom. Unless there's anything else someone would like to say, I'll be going now."

Clint noticed that the judge had already begun to walk down the hall, his footsteps smacking against the floor in a determined clatter. "Hey," Clint blurted out. "What about me?"

The clatter stopped. All Clint could see was the back of one of Judge Fountain's legs. His voice, however, boomed through the jail like trapped thunder. "Let him go, Sheriff. There's no reason to keep an innocent man behind bars."

Hesitating with the keys in one hand, the sheriff looked anxiously between the judge and Clint. "But shouldn't we wait until—"

"I've heard plenty," Fountain replied. "I trust the word of your deputy and that of Mister Garrett. Mister Adams won't be allowed to leave town, however, until this matter is resolved. Understood?"

"Yes, sir," Clint said.

"Then that's the last of it. Open that cell and let Mister Adams out so he can rest up for the trial. It might be a while before this matter comes to a close, so he might as well wait in the comfort every free man should enjoy."

FIFTEEN

The judge's legs disappeared from Clint's view and Fountain's steps echoed down the hall, followed by the sound of the jail's door opening and closing. Although the sheriff didn't look entirely happy about the decision, he fit a key into the lock of Clint's cell and twisted it inside the mechanism. The door swung open and Clint walked outside.

"You heard Judge Fountain," the sheriff said sternly. "You're not to leave town until this case is closed, understand?"

Clint nodded. "I sure do."

"I'll still have to keep your gun with me. You'll get it back when this clears up."

Although he didn't like that too much, Clint wasn't surprised about it either.

"Now get on out of here, Adams."

Clint walked behind the lawmen and next to Pat Garrett. The sheriff all but threw the rest of Clint's belongings at him, making sure to lock away the Colt and gun belt in a cabinet along with the rest of his rifles and pistols.

Garrett tipped his hat to the other men and followed Clint outside. "Sorry about your gun. I can talk to Sheriff Pickering about getting it back for you after he cools down a bit. He gets

63

his feathers ruffled when the judge comes in and orders him around like that."

"Don't worry about it, Mister Garrett. Not having a gun sure beats the hell out of spending another day sitting on that go-dawful bench." Besides which, Clint knew he had another gun—his Colt New Line—in his room.

"When word gets out that you're out and about, you might be needing that gun of yours quicker than you think. And by the way, call me Pat."

Clint looked over at the ex-lawman. Garrett stood a few inches taller than him and had the stern, hardened features of a man who'd forged through a lifetime of fighting for one reason or another. Outside of the dim shadows of a saloon and without the hectic tension surrounding a gunfight, Clint could get a clearer look at Pat Garrett and see him without the intrusion of any other factors.

Garrett had the build of a boxer and the reserved demeanor of someone who was used to being listened to and relied upon. The well-kept mustache over his upper lip was thick and graying in spots just like the dark, sandy hair on top of his head. But what struck Clint most about the man was his eyes. They peered out at the world as if they were quietly studying every face and every detail. There was strength in those eyes that ran all the way down to the core of his soul.

"So do you think there's going to be trouble from Drezdev and his friends?" Clint asked.

"Well, they're not the sophisticated types. Normally, they stick to robbing small stores in other towns or extortion schemes. Never anything like this that takes more than a few minutes to think out. Therefore, it's pretty safe to say that they got something bigger planned."

"Great," Clint said as his hand went for the empty space at his side where his modified Colt usually rested. "And I'm not exactly prepared for anything bigger."

"I got a look at that piece you carry. It's a fine bit of crafts-manship."

"Thanks, but it doesn't do me a whole lot of good sitting in the sheriff's office. And after the way he was looking at me, I think it'd be best if I tried to keep my distance from there for a while."

Garrett nodded. "You're probably right about that. Here," he said as he drew his own weapon and offered it handle-first to Clint. "Why don't you keep this with you in case you run into trouble."

As soon as the gun touched Clint's hand, thoughts ran through his mind centering on all the legends that had been building around Pat Garrett. Although many of them were far from complimentary, they involved names of figures like Arkansas Dave Rudabaugh and the Lincoln County War. All of that and plenty more existed under the looming shadow of one William Bonney, know to the world and history as Billy the Kid.

The Kid ran a campaign death throughout the southwest that somehow got a lot of people thinking Bonney was some kind of hero. Clint wasn't about to pass judgment on the dead, but it was undisputed fact that the Kid was a killer who'd met his end at the hand of the man standing in front of him right now.

Some say Pat Garrett was a great lawman who took on an impossible job and saw it through to the end, doing everything that needed to be done to get there. Unfortunately, with the Kid's legend being what it was, Garrett was seen by most as a traitorous coward who'd known Billy for several years before shooting him in the back inside a meat locker in Fort Sumner.

From what Clint had seen of the man, it was hard to picture Pat Garrett as someone that would sneak up on an old friend and put a bullet into him just to make a few dollars and a feeble attempt at fame. Instead, Clint was starting to see some of the torture going on inside Garrett's head. It showed through in those hard, unflinching eyes that reflected a burden on his soul that had been there since that night in Fort Sumner.

Clint took Garrett's gun and held it carefully in one hand. "Are you sure about this? I mean . . . you were there, too. They might be coming after you just like they might be coming after me."

Garrett shrugged dismissively. "Don't fret it, Adams. I've run into them more than once. They know better than to get on my bad side. In fact, I'm sure they know about you, too. That's probably why they wanted to . . ."

Freezing in mid-sentence, Garrett looked down the street with widening eyes and then back at Clint. "That's it," he said. "That's what they were trying to do."

Clint was about to ask Garrett what he was talking about when a notion hit him that stopped the breath before it made it out of his lungs. "You said they were getting ready for something big. Something bigger than they've tried before."

"That's right," Garrett said as he began walking at a quick pace down the boardwalk.

After a few jogging steps, Clint was striding right beside the ex-lawman. "Even a fool would know that they wouldn't be able to get a man hung by just threatening a few witnesses and lying to the sheriff. So that means they just wanted to get us out of the way."

Garrett nodded. His eyes narrowed into intense slits and he walked just a little bit faster down the street. "Right again. All they needed was to get you into a cell for a little while. They know me well enough to be sure that I'd probably try to help you out if I could, so that keeps both of us and the sheriff busy."

"And whatever they've got planned," Clint said. "It's set to go off real soon."

"If it hasn't happened already." Suddenly, Garrett stopped and turned to look Clint square in the eyes. "You can still walk away from this, Adams. I know Drezdev and Carlyle well enough to figure out where they might be headed, but I don't think we have enough time to explain it to the sheriff. I could use your help, but if you don't want to get involved, I under—"

"Stop right there, Pat. You helped me and I'll be happy to return the favor. Besides," Clint said, "I owe this Drezdev something for w¹at he's done to me. I don't much appreciate being locked up in a cage."

"Then it's settled," Garrett said with a grin that eased onto him like an old faded hat. "I'm headed back to my house for another gun and then we can look for Drezdev. Why don't you start at the general store and work your way toward the bank. He's been bragging about a big robbery for some time now and that's where he might start. I'll catch up with you before too long."

Clint still held the borrowed gun in one hand, almost as though he was afraid of damaging it. "Does Drezdev know about how quickly Judge Fountain works?"

"Not from personal experience, that's for sure. The judge usually does his best to keep the likes of him inside that jail rather than out of it."

"Then he might not be expecting me to be out so soon. I'll see if I can catch up to them, but won't make the first move. Once we get them in our sights, you take the lead and I'll keep my head down somewhere out of sight. That way, we can take advantage of the edge Judge Fountain's given us."

"Well, I'll head to the store first. As much as Drezdev might want to hit the bank, he might not be ready for it just yet. Give me a signal to let me know you're nearby and I'll move in."

Garrett turned and started back down the street. Clint stepped into an alleyway with the notion of cutting over a few blocks to head in the direction of the general store. He paused for a second, making sure that nobody else was around to see he was there. "Hey Pat," he said just loud enough to be heard.

Turning, Garrett stopped and looked over his shoulder.

Clint stepped into the light, thinking about all he'd heard about the ex-lawman. There were so many rumors and stories around him that it was hard to see Garrett as just a man made out of flesh and bone. Somehow, the rumors of disgrace and cowardice just didn't fit upon Pat Garrett's shoulders.

"It's good to be working with you," Clint said.

Garrett nodded once and turned to leave. Even so, Clint was able to spot a glimmer of pride in his eyes that shone like a coin that had been forgotten at the bottom of a well.

SIXTEEN

None of the others that Drezdev and Carlyle ambushed put up as much of a struggle as Ben from the Split Hitch. That was the reason the outlaws had gone to the bartender first, so that the most difficult target would be put down before any of the others.

With Ben gone, the owner of the general store and the bank president fell like dominoes. One after another, the businessmen were snatched from their homes or outside of their own offices so they could be trussed up and thrown into a dark place next to their fellow hostages. All of the victims sported bruises on their faces and lumps on their heads, but were still well enough to draw a breath. Ben sat slumped over in a corner of their makeshift prison, beaten more severely than the others and unable to move a muscle.

In the space of an hour, Drezdev and Carlyle stood outside a barn belonging to Krow's uncle and looked at each other victoriously.

"The hard part's over," Carlyle said. "All that's left is for us to get back into town and collect our money."

Drezdev and Carlyle both wore double-rig holsters around their waists. Carlyle brandished a belt of ammunition slug over one shoulder even though they had yet to fire a shot. Both men simply felt better having the weapons at their disposal. It made no difference to them that so far they had only gone up against the likes of bankers, clerks and bartenders.

After spending a few seconds congratulating each other, the two outlaws climbed onto their horses and started riding back to town. Krow's barn was less than a mile away, but they rode as if their horses' tails were on fire. Hooves thundered over packed ground and their voices shattered the air as they hollered to celebrate an early victory, certain that there was nobody to stand in their way.

They made it back into White Sands with time to spare. Drezdev reined in his horse and turned the animal toward the bank. "You head down to the store and close it up. I'll do the same at the bank. Meet me there and we'll start at the top. By the time we work our way down, we'll have enough money to get out of here and live like kings for years."

"What about Krow?" Carlyle asked.

"What about him?"

"He was supposed to be in on this deal all the way to the end. I can pick him up at the doc's and maybe he can be a scout or—"

"To hell with Krow! That stupid bastard couldn't even keep from getting his dumb ass shot. We don't need the likes of him on this job. Hell, we got everything wrapped up so tight that my brother's kids could rob these places. Krow can sit and play with himself for all I care. Maybe that'd give him some time to think about what a screw-up he is."

Carlyle stared intently toward the other end of town where Krow was resting at that very moment. He'd been the one to try and take his partner out of the doctor's care so the plan could move ahead with all three of them just like it was supposed to. But after a few hours, Krow's wound had started to bleed so heavily that it soaked through every dressing they'd tried to put on it. When they'd dropped him off back at the doctor, Drezdev spat on the ground and cursed Krow's name.

"This ain't right," Carlyle said. "Not by a flush."

Bringing his horse up alongside Carlyle's, Drezdev stared into his partner's eyes as though he was trying to set a fire inside the other man's skull. "What're you sayin'?" he growled.

"You tryin' to back out now when we're almost done with this? After we managed to get Adams and that piece of shit Garrett out of the way, you want to start bellyaching over Krow?"

"He's our partner, Mick. If it was you that got shot, we wouldn't leave you sitting without—"

Drezdev's hand flashed out to cover the distance between the two men like a rattlesnake lunging out to bite. The back of his fist smacked into Carlyle's face, making a sharp cracking sound that barely brought a wince to the other man's eyes.

"That's just to put some sense back into you," Drezdev said as Carlyle's hand went for his gun. "Krow wasn't good for nothin' besides thinking of ways to spend our money. That's all he's ever done and now that we got the biggest score of our lives, he gets himself shot. If we go after him now, we might catch the attention of a deputy or even the sheriff himself. Think for a second, goddammit! Use your brain for Christ's sake."

A seething fire burned behind Carlyle's eyes. But as the seconds ticked past, that fire died down a bit. It didn't fade away completely, but it did cool to a smoldering glow. His hand slid away from his gun and he choked back his rage. "You're right. Let's do this and get it over with."

"Right. We'll worry about Krow when we can."

Carlyle kept his eyes on Drezdev, even as the other man turned his horse around and rode down the street. Already, he was making plans and figuring out new angles that would take him in directions that he'd never even considered until just this moment. The last two minutes had taught Carlyle a hell of a lot.

The lesson consisted of three simple words: Don't trust anybody.

SEVENTEEN

Although Clint was new to White Sands, he'd seen enough of the town to know where the general store and bank were located. After spending so many years passing through from town to town, his mind had become accustomed to automatically looking for the important landmarks. There was always a need for a store and the bank usually marked the center of the business district, which made them both stand out clearly in his mind.

Clint stuck to the alleys and back streets whenever he could, darting between buildings with his head down and his hat pulled over his eyes. For the most part, folks passing by didn't seem to pay him much mind. Besides the occasional sideways glance or word of greeting, he might as well have been just another part of the scenery.

After being locked up in a cage and talking to Judge Fountain, being another part of the background was becoming more and more familiar to Clint. At the moment, however, that was exactly the way he wanted it.

There was no activity at or around the bank. Even though it was the middle of the day, Clint couldn't spot one person walking into or out of the building. He didn't have a lot of time to wait around, but Clint picked a spot on a corner and stood there for a minute. Without trying to look conspicuous, he watched the bank as well as the people who passed it, looking for a sign of anything out of the ordinary.

Then, just as he was about to move on, Clint spotted something that put it all into perspective. It wasn't much. Just a solitary man who walked up to the bank's door and pulled on the handle. When the door didn't budge, he looked inside, shrugged and walked on down the street.

Clint waited for the man to get out of sight before he walked up to the bank to have a look for himself. Sure enough, the sign hanging from the inside of the door read CLOSED despite the fact that there was no holiday or any other reason for business to stop that day. He peeked inside through a pane of glass fitted into the door and couldn't see a living soul inside that bank.

For a moment, Clint had been expecting to see rows of people sitting on the floor with their hands in the air and the gunmen stuffing money into their pockets behind the counter. But the truth was much less dramatic. There was simply . . . nothing.

Not wanting to waste more time than necessary, Clint shoved his hands into his pockets and walked briskly toward the general store, which was only a block away. He couldn't decide what to make out of the bank situation, or even if he should make anything out of it at all. What he did know was that Garrett would be heading for the general store and he would be expecting backup.

Clint did not want to disappoint him.

When he got to the general store, Clint found a very familiar scene. Once again, there was nobody around the place even though it was the middle of the business day. There was nobody walking to or from the store and nobody walking in or out of it. The only thing Clint could see was the faintest hint of movement coming from inside the store itself.

That, at least, was something different than what he'd seen before.

As much as he wanted to creep up to the front of the store and look inside, he was afraid that even something like that might be enough to blow the surprise that he and Garrett had cooked up for the outlaws. After all, it would only require a quick glimpse of Clint's face to put Drezdev or Carlyle on their guard. And once that happened, he might as well just stand up and walk straight at them.

Clint stood in an alleyway directly across the street from the store, keeping himself hidden behind a stack of empty crates in the shadow cast by a squat, two-story building. The crates were old shipping boxes with every other plank missing, which made it perfect for him to see through without being seen himself.

The instant he'd seen the movement inside the store, he'd drawn his borrowed gun and snapped back the hammer. And just as he was starting to get overly anxious, Clint saw another source of movement coming from the boardwalk running in front of the store, itself. It was a figure making its way directly toward the store, walking at a leisurely pace while still keeping his steps light enough to make sure his boots hardly made a sound upon the occasional loose board.

Pat Garrett strode down the walkway, his hands held down close to his holster and his eyes on the lookout for anything that was headed in his direction. His tall, solid form moved with the subtle grace of a predator. Not one motion was wasted. Nothing he did gave any hint to his prey that he was coming for them.

Clint watched for a few seconds, wondering if this was how it had been when Garrett was tracking Billy the Kid. Now, more than ever, it was easy to tell that this was no ordinary man. Even among other lawmen, Garrett stood out from the rest simply by the way he took to naturally hunting his prey. Having hunted more than his own share of men, Clint knew what qualities made for a good hunter.

One of the most important was the ability to know when to charge in and when to stalk. The true hunter charged so quickly that the target never even saw what was coming at them until it was too late to do anything about it but absorb the damage of the assault. And when the hunter stalked his prey, he was practically invisible to them, even if he was walking in plain sight.

Such was the case with Garrett's approach to the general store. Somehow, he knew that Drezdev and Carlyle were in there. He knew they would be on their guard and ready for an attack.

It was time to stalk.

Garret did so without making so much as a single step known to the outlaws. In fact he practically got right up to the front of the store itself before Clint was able to send his signal. At the last second, however, Garrett stopped and took one more look around, almost as though he knew what Clint was thinking and where he was waiting.

Holding his borrowed pistol up into a beam of sunlight that had slipped through the cracks in the crate he was using for cover, Clint moved the gun back and forth slightly as the light glinted off the metal cylinder.

For a moment, Clint wasn't sure if Garrett saw the light winking at him from across the street. But then the ex-lawman held up a hand and waved in Clint's direction. He crept up toward the front of the store, turning at the last second so that he could press his back up against the building next to a large picture window beside the front door. Moving like a living shadow that worked its way unseen across the ground, Garrett scouted out what was happening inside the store and then worked his way back to the boardwalk.

From there, he immediately walked across the street toward the alley where Clint was waiting. Instinctually, he sought cover behind some of the clutter there and ducked behind a stack of empty barrels directly across from Clint's spot. Garrett looked over to the crates, saw Clint crouching in the shadows and nodded.

"Glad to see you could make it," Garrett said. "What did you find at the bank?"

Clint kept one eye on the store across the street and the other on the alley. "Not a lot. In fact, they were closed. By the looks of it, there hadn't been anyone there to open the doors at all this morning."

"That was the way it was over at the Split Hitch. Normally, they're open for the early crowd and a few who actually like the food. I'm a part of that last group and I sure would've known if they were going to be closed. Ben's usually pretty good about letting the regular customers know those things. Actually," Garrett said as a stray thought hit him right between the eyes, "I haven't seen Ben all day. Normally, I catch sight of him or the other bartender as they head over to open up the place."

"I'll be damned," Clint said to himself. Turning to Garrett, he felt as though he'd somehow managed to step back and get a look at the entire picture rather than just a few pieces of it up close. From his new perspective, it was much easier to see how every little thing fit together.

"Looks like you're thinking the same thing as me."

"Did you happen to catch sight of the people who would normally open the bank and general store?"

"Nope," Garrett replied. "And you are definitely on the same track as I am, since Drezdev would need to get his hands on those folks if he wanted to make off with a clean sweep by robbing those places in the middle of the day with as little fuss as possible."

Shaking his head, Clint almost felt a bit of admiration for the outlaws. "If they get their hands on the owners or managers of those businesses and get them to tell where they keep their money, safe combinations or anything else they might need, they could head over to those places and make sure nobody got inside to get in their way while they worked."

"It's always other workers or someone in the crowd that makes a robbery difficult," Garrett agreed. "By making sure they've got the place to themselves, a couple of thieves could be in and out in a few minutes."

"And with the help of the managers, they wouldn't even have to crack a safe, pick a lock or even kick down a door. Hell, they'd barely have to think to pull off a job like that once they'd taken the right people hostage."

"Sounds like the perfect job for Drezdev's bunch. They don't do too well if they have to think too hard," Garrett said as he stepped out from behind the barrels and drew his gun. "And you're right about one thing. They won't be expecting you to be on the loose this quickly." After checking to make sure the cylinder in his pistol was full, Garrett snapped it shut and stood to his full six feet four inches. "Give me a minute to announce myself, then join in. If I know Drezdev half as well as I think I do, that should be plenty of time to get him to fight."

Clint watched as Garrett strode across the street and right up to the front of the store. Now more than ever, he looked like a hungry predator wading into battle. The time for stalking was over.

It was time to charge.

EIGHTEEN

Drezdev and Carlyle took their own sweet time walking through the general store, taking what they wanted and hitting the two places that the owner had told them to look for hidden money. Since they'd made sure that the store was closed, they didn't have to worry about keeping customers quiet or even brandishing their guns. All of the hard work had been done already when they'd snatched the store owner from his home earlier that morning.

The middle-aged owner wasn't the type to fight when he was threatened with a gun in the brutally creative ways that Carlyle had come up with. Instead, he'd told the outlaws what they'd wanted to know so they would let him live a bit longer. After all, money could be replaced. Fingers, toes, arms, legs and life itself could not.

It was the same for the important men connected to the bank and saloon. After a bit of coaxing, they'd all cracked eventually. Some, however, would sport bigger scars than others.

For the time being, Drezdev and Carlyle were wrapping up their raid on the general store. They had about a hundred dollars to show for it as well as a crate full of supplies they'd be needing when they pulled out of town later that night.

"This was too damn easy," Carlyle said as he shoved some

of the money they'd stolen into his pocket. "How come we never thought about doing this before?"

"Because the bank's the first thing anyone ever thinks about when they're lookin' for someplace to rob. Last time I was in here to buy a saddle, I noticed how much money the owner of this place was sittin' on. Same thing with the Split Hitch."

"So what's next?"

"I'd say the bank. It's been long enough for word to spread that it's closed. We'll have to sneak in the back way, but there shouldn't be much of anyone poking around there anymore. If we wait too long, someone'll get suspicious enough to look for old man Johnston. If we go now, we can be in and out and on the trail before the heat gets too bad."

Carlyle slung a sack that he'd filled over his shoulder and walked toward the front door. He paused at the window next to it and took a look outside. In the next moment, he pulled his head away from the glass, dropped everything he was holding and grabbed for the gun strapped to his hip.

"What the hell's wrong with you?" Drezdev asked. Then he looked at the expression on his partner's face, which was more than enough to drain some of the color from his own skin. He, too, dropped what he was holding and made a dash for the space behind the counter. "Who's out there?"

"Take a look for yourself."

Walking in a low crouch that was almost comical from somebody with such a crooked back to begin with, Drezdev shuffled across the room toward the window.

There was a thin, filmy curtain hanging over the window that filtered out the light as if through a cloudy haze. Sunlight streamed into the store, casting a soft, golden glow into the air. Blotting out the light and moving across the floor was a tall, looming shadow that swept forward into the store to take the form of a slender man with his arms held down at his sides.

Drezdev used the barrel of his gun to pull aside a piece of the curtain so he could see who was walking right up to the front of the store as if he owned the place. When he looked out, Pat Garrett's eyes were looking straight back at him, slicing right through the glass to send a jolt into Drezdev's gut and the rest of him backpedaling away from the window.

"What the hell is he doing here?" Drezdev said in a low snarl.

"Maybe one of the hostages got free."

Drezdev raised his gun and snapped the hammer back. "Stuff all the money into one sack. We'll come back for the rest of it later."

"Come back? We'll be lucky to get out of here at all!"

"Just shut up and do it. I'll make sure we get out of here if I have to blast a hole through that cowardly son of a bitch to do it."

Moving away from the front wall, Drezdev aimed his gun at the window and started squeezing off rounds through the large piece of plate glass. The curtain twitched and writhed like a tortured spirit as lead ripped through the material and punched holes through to the other side. Shards of glass flew out toward the street, creating a brilliant reflective mist that caught the sunlight and tossed it in hundreds of different directions at once.

After consolidating all the money and most valuable items into one sack, Carlyle hefted the bag over his shoulder and drew his own gun. Relying solely on the panic-fueled instinct that ran rampant through his system at that moment, he pointed his weapon in the direction of his enemy and sent as many bullets as he could toward the shadowy figure in the shortest amount of time as possible.

For the next few seconds, all either man could hear was the explosive voices of their weapons and the shattering of glass, which echoed through the store like sharp, stinging thunder. Even after they stopped shooting, the ringing in their ears droned on, accompanied by the occasional piece of glass falling from the frame to break when it hit the floor.

When all of that died away and the two men stood frozen with their guns in their hands enclosed in a mist of acrid smoke, Drezdev slowly reached for the spare bullets on his gun belt and looked hesitantly over to Carlyle. "That must've killed him."

"Then we'd better get out of here."

"Why don't you check just to make sure?"

Snapping his wrist to expose the pistol's chamber, Carlyle

flicked out the empty cartridges and slid in fresh ones. "I'm not that stupid. You check."

Suddenly, both men heard something that stopped them even before they could develop the argument any further. It wasn't anything too dramatic or even very loud. Just the sound of heavy footsteps ... slowly pounding on the boardwalk approaching the entrance to the store.

Drezdev quickly reloaded his weapon and moved around behind the counter, which had a recently emptied cash register on one end. "It's Garrett," he said quickly. "How the hell did he know to come here?"

"Hell if I know. Last I heard, he was over at the sheriff's trying to get Adams out of jail."

"There ain't no way he could've done that so quickly. Not with a hard-ass like Fountain on the case."

The footsteps were almost to the front door now. When they stopped, so did the breath of both outlaws standing inside the store. They gripped their guns and reloaded as quick as their trembling fingers could manage. When they snapped the chambers closed, some of their courage seeped back into their bodies.

"You ready?" Drezdev asked with a look of grim determination etched across his face.

Carlyle nodded.

"Then let's put that bastard into the ground."

NINETEEN

Clint stayed behind the pile of crates, fighting back the urge to run out of the alley and go to Garrett's side. It wasn't because he had little faith in the man, but Clint still didn't like to see anyone walking right up to a couple of desperate men who had no qualms about killing. Especially when those men were caught red-handed in the middle of the crime they'd thought was foolproof.

Still, he knew that Garrett would be relying on him to wait through his entire minute before revealing himself. Whatever the ex-lawman had planned, Clint would just have to stand by and watch it come to pass.

Garrett strode across the street and up the short walk that led to the front of the store. The seconds ticked by on leaden feet and every instinct in Clint's mind cried out to yell at Garrett to duck from the gunfire that was sure to come at any second. Then, almost as if Garrett had heard Clint's mental warnings, the tall figure hopped off the boardwalk and spun his body in a tight half-circle, which put him behind a large tree in front of the store.

The shots blasted through the air, shattering glass and whipping through the space that had only just been left behind by Garrett. Clint pulled himself down and behind the crates as stray rounds ricocheted off the alley's entrance and chewed into the edge of his cover. Although the barrage only lasted a few seconds, Clint felt as though he'd left Garrett behind for hours and when the shooting stopped, the countdown in the back of his mind reached zero.

It had been a minute.

Now was the time to even out the odds.

Clint took a quick look around the crates just to make sure he wasn't about to charge head-first into a meat grinder. He saw no movement coming from the store so he bolted from the alley and made his way over to the tree where Garrett had sought cover. To his surprise, Clint didn't see Garrett by that tree. Instead, the ex-lawman was back on the boardwalk leading to the front door, his hand poised on the handle as though he was just about to step inside for some cooking supplies.

The instant Clint's foot touched the boardwalk, Garrett raised his hand and motioned for him to step to the side. Without looking over his shoulder, Garrett grabbed hold of the door's handle, tugged it open and threw himself against the wall between the door and what was left of the window.

Clint reflexively dove to the side, aiming his body for the solid tree that had done such a good job of providing cover for Garrett. He knew what was coming just as much as the ex-lawman and made sure he was ready for it by keeping as much of himself as possible behind the tree's thick trunk.

Another wave of gunfire erupted from inside the store, this time more focused and not quite as wild. After five or six shots whipped through the air taking chunks from the door frame, they stopped.

As far as he could tell, it looked as though the men inside the store weren't aware that they had two targets to worry about instead of just one. None of the shots fired had come in Clint's direction, although that could just as well mean that the outlaws weren't very good with their aim. Clint edged around the tree just enough so he could look around the trunk and see what Garrett was doing.

The ex-lawman stood with his back pressed against the wall, thumbing back the hammer on his gun. Clint reminded himself that he was using a borrowed weapon and snapped back his own hammer as well. Crouching down low, Clint peered cautiously toward the storefront. He kept his arm tight against the tree so that only his pistol broke from cover.

In one fluid motion, Garrett pushed himself away from the wall and over to one side, heading for the window rather than the door. As he went past the broken pane, he pumped a few shots into the store and kept right on moving until he was standing against the opposite edge of the building.

Clint could hear hurried footsteps thumping within the store as well as a couple of voices speaking in hurried whispers. The footsteps were coming straight for the window. Hearing this, Garrett waited a second or two until one of the outlaws stuck his head out and brought his gun up to take a few shots. From what he could see, Clint recognized the outlaw as Tom Carlyle.

Spinning in a tight arc, Garrett squeezed off another round, which punched into the window's frame hard enough to send a shower of splinters down on top of the outlaw's head. He then dove around the corner just as Carlyle's bullets whipped through the air.

The outlaw watched as Garrett took off around the corner, leaning out of the window as far as he could without falling facefirst out of the building.

Clint smiled slightly as he watched the gutsy maneuver that placed Carlyle in perfect position to be picked off by someone waiting in just the right place. That place was right about where Clint was standing at that moment. The fact that he and Carlyle were so perfectly positioned at this moment was only a testament to how far ahead Garrett had planned this exact scenario.

"Hey!" Clint barked as he sighted down the barrel of his pistol.

Carlyle instinctively snapped his head around in response to the unexpected voice. The instant he saw Clint staring back at him from behind the tree, Carlyle swung his gun around while desperately trying to pull himself back inside the store.

With the amount of time Carlyle was in his sights, Clint would have been able to shoot him six times, reload, and then shoot him again. As it was, one shot was all he needed. The pistol bucked in Clint's hand and drilled a piece of hot lead into the outlaw's chest, knocking him off his feet sideways, slamming his back against a shard of glass that hung in the window frame like a huge, crystalline tooth.

The glass stabbed into Carlyle's back, sliding in like a greased dagger between his shoulder blades and through the tough layers of muscle beneath his flesh. Enough pain washed through him to wipe away the agony caused by Clint's bullet. As his momentum drove the glass in farther, that agony reached such intense levels that it burned out of his system entirely, leaving the outlaw's body numb as a slab of dead meat.

Carlyle's face contorted in a mask of blind rage. His gun went off in his hand, but his arm was suddenly too heavy to lift. The gun blasted once, sending its round into the floor while Carlyle pitched himself sideways to land with a solid *thump* inside the store.

Clint sprung forward and rushed past the window in a low crouch. With his adrenaline surging through his body and brain, he wasn't even sure if any shots came at him from inside the building. Instead, he pressed his back against the wall and turned toward the corner.

"It's me. Don't shoot," Clint said right before taking a look around the corner.

But the ex-lawman was gone. And when Clint turned to get a look at the front of the store, so was Carlyle.

Clint felt his heart beating like a savage drum in his chest. Taking a second to think, Clint decided to not waste time looking for Garrett. Instead, he would anticipate what the man's next move would be and what would be the best way to complement it. He drew in a breath and got ready to stampede through the window, hoping that he'd guessed correctly.

TWENTY

Drezdev was half a second away from running to his partner's side when Carlyle leaned out the window to take his shots at Garrett. But then he'd heard that one word, shouted from the wrong direction. After that, Carlyle was knocked back and into the broken piece of glass, his back and chest awash in blood, which spewed from him like a geyser beneath his clothes.

Poised less than a foot away from being able to see out the window to where the shot had come from, Drezdev threw himself to the floor and sent a couple of rounds through the wall. He wasn't sure if he'd hit anything or not. He wasn't even exactly sure who he was shooting at or where his target was. All he knew was that he had to do something before this entire job went any further south than it already had.

Even bearing two fresh wounds, Carlyle hit the floor with fire blazing brightly behind his eyes, almost as though he'd found some way to put the pain aside and see this fight through to the end. The boards beneath him turned slick with blood, which quickly soaked in to the wood, turning it a dark, murky black.

"Hang on, Tom," Drezdev shouted as he reached out to grab hold of Carlyle's shoulder. "This ain't over yet!"

• • •

Clint heard those words over the ringing in his ears. He could also hear another set of heavy footsteps shuffling inside the store, letting him know that there was still plenty more to do before this day was through. The shots that had dug holes in the wall were a little high and buried themselves deeply into the tree that had served himself and Garrett so well. Ignoring the wild shots, Clint kept his head low and moved in closer to the store.

As far as he could tell, Drezdev hadn't seen him run past the window. Either Carlyle was blocking the other man's view or Drezdev was just too rattled to notice much of anything besides the gunfire echoing in his ears and the blood covering his friend's body. Clint decided to press his advantage and got ready to charge through the broken window, hoping that Drezdev was still looking toward the tree rather than at him.

He thumbed back the hammer of his pistol as he pushed away from the wall and swung himself around in a tight semi-circle, which faced him toward the bullet-riddled storefront. Running on sheer primal instinct, Clint lowered his head and took a leaping step through the shattered window frame.

His boot landed with a wet crunch on a thin layer of blood and broken glass. Clint's eyes took in his new surroundings in less than a second while his arm came up to point his gun at the closest target he could see. Carlyle was moving, but still on his back, so that left Drezdev as his biggest threat.

Clint's hand flashed through the air, bringing the pistol up to bear on Drezdev. But even as he got ready to pull his trigger, he saw the outlaw already had his gun up and ready and was about to take his shot.

With the counter on his left and Carlyle laying stretched out directly in front of him, Clint was fresh out of clear paths to take. Since he didn't have much time to think on the matter, he kept his momentum rolling and launched into a leaping step that would take him over Carlyle and closer to a row of shelves carrying various dry goods.

As Clint jumped over Carlyle's body, Drezdev's gun exploded and sent a bullet toward Clint that might have struck flesh if Clint had stopped moving even for an instant after entering the store. As it was, the bullet tore through the air and slammed into the wall, where it buried into one of the studs supporting the front of the building. Another shot followed directly after that one, but only managed to chip off a piece of broken glass before sailing skyward.

Clint's boot touched down onto the floor and he immediately began twisting his body to line up his gun with Drezdev. But instead of following behind the rest of him, Clint's other foot stopped abruptly within a desperate, vice-like grip. The sudden halt nearly dropped Clint flat onto his face, but his reflexes kicked in just in time to shift his weight so he could stay up on one leg.

It wasn't the most attractive of landings, but it kept him from falling into Drezdev's mercy after being pulled off his feet. Clint twisted around to look over his shoulder and he saw that Carlyle himself had dredged up enough strength to reach up and pluck him from the air. The wounded man had also managed to hold onto his gun. Glaring up at him with fatal determination in his eyes, Carlyle struggled to lift the hand bearing the weight of his pistol.

Even though the big man on the floor moved as though he was nailed to it, Carlyle only had to move his hand an inch or so before he could point his gun directly at Clint's chest. With one last twitch, Carlyle wrenched his upper body around and clenched his teeth together in pain as the glass stake was driven even farther into his back. Even so, he'd managed to bring his gun up to fire while Clint still struggled to regain his balance.

The gunshot blasted through the store, echoing off the nearby shelves like a cannon, followed by the sickening thump of lead impacting against flesh and bone.

Clint's gun hadn't made it up to fire and he didn't even have enough time to throw himself down and out of the way. His eyes reflexively snapped shut and when he opened them again, he looked down to see where he'd been hit.

"Jesus," Carlyle grunted through a mouthful of blood.

The grip around Clint's ankle went slack, allowing him to get both feet underneath him and secure his stance. Using his free hand to pat himself down for injuries, Clint scanned the room to see what had just happened. The first thing he saw was Carlyle laying on the floor, staring blankly up at the ceiling.

Next, Clint saw Pat Garrett toward the back of the room, his gun in hand and still smoking after having just been fired.

It was at that moment that Clint knew he hadn't been hit. Instead, that last gunshot had put Carlyle out of his misery less than a second before Clint had come face to face with his creator.

"Don't even think about it, Drezdev," Garrett warned.

Clint looked toward the window and spotted Drezdev as he stopped with one foot poised in the window frame. The outlaw pulled himself back into the store and wheeled around to face Clint and Garrett.

Garrett's voice was a low, menacing rumble. "Don't make me kill you, too."

Drezdev kept looking between both men, occasionally glancing down at the body of his partner. Already, Carlyle looked less like a man and more like something that had been drained of all its vital ingredients. Eyes open and clothes soaked with blood, the shell that had once been Tom Carlyle laid discarded on the floor.

"You—you son of a bitch," Drezdev snarled. Looking to Garrett, he said, "It's true. All of it's true. You'd shoot a dying man before fighting someone on their feet and facing you. When were you gonna kill me? Were you gonna wait till my back was turned, you cowardly bas—"

The outlaw's words were cut off as Clint stepped over to him and pounded the butt of his gun against the side of his skull. Drezdev wobbled in his spot for a second and then dropped straight back to land on the ground outside the store.

"That was more bullshit than I could stomach," Clint said.

TWENTY-ONE

"So what the hell am I supposed to think about all of this?" Sheriff Pickering walked back and forth in front of the general store as though he was about to start pulling his hair out at the roots. "Could somebody answer that for me?"

Pat Garrett leaned up against the tree, which now looked like it had been chewed on by some angry rodents. "If I was in your shoes I'd thank myself and Mister Adams for doing your job for you."

The look Sheriff Pickering shot over to Garrett was nearly harsh enough to dig another hole into that old tree. After fixing Clint with a similar gaze, the lawman strode over to Garrett and dragged him to the side by the elbow. "What in blazes has gotten into you, Pat? Have you lost all the sense that you were born with?"

Clint turned his back on Garrett and the sheriff. Walking into the store, he stepped up to where the deputies had gathered in a small circle around Drezdev. The outlaw was still a bit groggy after waking up from his painful nap, which had made it that much easier for the deputies to shackle his wrists together with a pair of bulky handcuffs.

Dave, the same one who'd allowed Alison to have her visit in the prison, did his best to put on the same tough expression that seemed to be permanently molded onto the sheriff's face. "What are you doing in here, Adams?"

"Just thought I'd like to come in through the front door for a change, that's all. Has he said anything yet?" Clint asked, nodding his head toward Drezdev.

"We'll be lucky if he remembers his name after that knock to the head he took. We might've been able to hear from Carlyle if Mister Garrett hadn't gone and—"

"Don't finish that sentence," Clint warned, using a voice that made the sheriff's seem like a friendly invitation to dinner. "If it wasn't for Pat Garrett, I might be dead right about now, so I won't hear him get bad-mouthed by anybody." Pressing the tip of his finger against the badge pinned to Dave's chest, Clint added, "And I do mean *anybody*."

Dave looked as though he was considering saying something if only to save face in front of the two other deputies looking on, but thought better of it when he took another look at Clint's face. "We found a broken strongbox and plenty of money stuffed into that one's pockets," he said, pointing over to Carlyle's body. "Looks like they was robbing this place."

"Wasn't there someone else who rode with Drezdev?" Clint asked.

"There sure was. His name's Will Krow and he's the one you shot over at the Split Hitch."

"So he's at the doctor's office? Or laying in bed somewhere?"

"I guess."

Clint glanced over to Drezdev and saw some of the lights coming back on behind the outlaw's eyes. "Since his friends decided to go on their little spree, shouldn't someone go and check out what Krow's up to?"

The deputy turned to face Clint head-on, drawing himself up to as tall as his legs could make him. "Look, you think you know so much better than us, why don't you just ask him whatever you want?" He took one step to the side and indicated Drezdev with a sweeping motion of his hand.

"Perfect," Clint said as he rubbed his hands together and crouched down to Drezdev's level. "Don't mind if I do."

∙   ∙   ∙

Sheriff Pickering only walked a few feet away from the store-front, putting just enough space between himself and the rest of his men to get some privacy. Garrett followed close behind, but made it plain that he was doing so out of his own accord rather than out of any fear or respect for the lawman.

"We've known each other a long time, Pat," the sheriff said in a lower voice. "And despite what everyone says about you, I've always given you the benefit of the doubt. Especially when it comes to legal matters."

"That's funny," Garrett replied. "The way I remember it, you were always the one who came to me when you needed help." Pausing just long enough to fix the sheriff with a hard stare, he added, "Especially when it came to legal matters."

"I might have requested your assistance a time or two, but that doesn't entitle you to any special favors."

"I don't remember asking for any favors."

Choking back a halfhearted laugh, the sheriff turned around to face the decimated remains of the general store. "I bring in your friend over there no less than a day ago for shooting a man dead in the saloon. You get Judge Fountain convinced to let him go and now I'm standing in front of another dead body. If you don't want me to throw your friend back into his cell just for being a royal pain in my ass, then you're asking for a mighty big favor indeed."

"You're right. I guess I should've just stood back and let them two rob this place and lord only knows how many others. Or maybe I should've come to you so you could tell me to mind my own business." With his teeth gnashed together in a fierce grimace, Garrett said, "I ain't your goddamn dog, Pick-ering. No matter how much you or this whole fucking town treats me like one, I ain't nobody's dog.

"There's no problem at all in calling on me when you need help finding a man that's running from the law or riding on a posse to bring in a killer or even a whole gang of them. But when I actually take down pieces of dogshit like those two in there, you have the nerve to give me hell for it?"

Unaffected by the grim resolve that showed through in Gar-rett's features, the sheriff stepped up until he was practically nose to nose with the other man. "In case you forgot, you ain't a lawman no more, Pat. And as much as I appreciate the help you've given in the past, I can't condone you going off on your own like this. Not when a man dies because of it."

Garrett nodded slowly. His mouth turned down into a thin slit of a frown. His eyes smoldered like embers burning deep inside his head. He stared right through to the back of Pickering's head until the sheriff finally averted his eyes and took a step back.

"If you try to arrest Clint Adams," Garrett said calmly, "I'll do my damndest to make sure you lose your job as sheriff in such a way that you'll want to forget what that badge looks like. And if you let that hunchbacked vermin out of your jail cell, I'll track him down and put a bullet in him myself."

Garrett slowly turned and walked toward the street.

"Where you going, Pat?" the sheriff asked. When he got no answer, he raised his voice, but refused to go chasing after him. "I still need to ask you some questions about what happened here."

"Ask your questions to Adams," Garrett said over his shoulder. "He's got no reason to lie to you."

"Where will I be able to find you?"

Without breaking stride, Garrett said, "Don't bother. I'm through with all of this. I'm through with everything."

TWENTY-TWO

When Drezdev opened his eyes, the first thing he saw was Clint Adams looking straight back at him. The outlaw's first instinct was to jump to his feet, but the moment he tried to move, Clint's boot put him right back in his place. His next impulse was to take a swing at Clint, but since his hands were shackled together as well as to the leg of a nearby table, he didn't have a lot of luck with that one either.

"You through yet?" Clint asked after Drezdev finally ran out of steam and slumped back down.

The outlaw sat on the floor with his back propped up against the same table he was chained to. His face was coated with thick layers of dust and gun smoke that gave his skin a decidedly gray, ashen hue, which made him look like something that had been pulled out from beneath a rock. When he started to speak in a rambling cascade of syllables, Drezdev's teeth clenched together and his lips twitched as though they were in spasm.

"I got nothing to say to you," Drezdev grunted. Although those weren't the first words he spoke, they were definitely the first ones Clint could understand.

"Oh, I think you do. At least, you would if you had any idea about what was good for you." Leaning in a little closer, Clint dropped his voice to a whisper. "You see, the sheriff doesn't want anything to do with you and the judge would just as soon hang you as look in your direction."

"So what? I guess I got nothin' to lose. So get out of my sight, Adams, before I get mad and decide to finish you off."

Nodding, Clint moved back for a second and then turned to smack his hand against the large, discolored knot on the side of Drezdev's temple. He didn't hit him that hard, but the bump was so sensitive that the slight contact nearly knocked the outlaw completely unconscious.

"That's just a reminder," Clint said. "It seems like you forgot who came out ahead in our little scuffle here today. Or, maybe you should ask your friend over there who's got the right to make any threats."

Clint stepped aside so Drezdev could look at Carlyle's body. The corpse still lay where it had landed. It was covered with a sheet that had been taken from one of the shelves. What had started out as white linen was now soaked through with so much blood that it stuck to Carlyle's body like an ill-fitting second skin. The smell of death still hung heavy in the air.

Suddenly, the rest of Drezdev's comments dried up in the back of his throat. Rather than spout off any more, he pitched himself back against the table hard enough to push the entire piece of furniture a few inches across the floor. He tried crossing his arms defiantly, but was denied even that simple statement by the shackles on his wrists.

"In case you haven't noticed," Clint said while taking a slow look around the store, "the sheriff's busy right now and the deputies have seen their way clear to taking a little walk for a minute or two. And that leaves me with plenty of time to finish the job I started and save the hangman a little elbow grease."

"What are you gettin' at?"

"Tell me where your hostages are."

"What hostages?"

Clint's fist snapped out like a bolt of lightning to rap unceremoniously on Drezdev's wounded skull. The outlaw barely saw the motion before a wave of pain rattled him right down to the bone.

"One more answer I don't like and I'll drop you on the floor right next to your friend. And trust me when I tell you that you'll have about as much luck getting up as he did." Clint let that sink in and then continued. "I passed by the bank. It was closed up just like this place. You knew right where to go to find where the money was hidden, which means you've had time to question the owner. You've probably got the owner of this place and others stashed somewhere. Even you wouldn't be dumb enough to kill them before the job was done. Tell me where they are and I'll let the judge know you started growing a conscience."

Drezdev shook his head. Although he was obviously in pain, it was the sight of Carlyle's body that seemed to shake him up even more. The grisly reality represented by that corpse was too tough of an argument for the outlaw to refute.

Finally, Drezdev lowered his eyes and muttered, "Krow's got a barn. It's on the outskirts of town. Ask him about it. He'll tell you where it is."

Clint backed off and motioned for the deputy to come back. Dave took his time, but didn't take enough to keep Clint waiting.

"You know where Krow's barn is?" Clint asked.

Dave thought and then nodded. "Yeah. I'm pretty sure I know where it is."

"Then let me take one or two of your men with me while I check it out. Something tells me we won't be disappointed."

Walking out the front door, Clint couldn't help but feel pleased with himself. After all, he and Garrett had managed to wrap up this little scheme Drezdev had cooked up without too much hassle. Now, hopefully, they could get to the hostages before anything happened to them.

Hoping that Garrett's name would be cleaned up a bit after such a successful job, Clint went outside and looked for the ex-lawman. All he could find was a very displeased Sheriff Pickering.

"Where's Mister Garrett?" Clint asked.

"Turned tail and ran," the sheriff said distastefully. "That's all he's good for, anyway."

Clint looked up and down the street, but could find no trace of Pat Garrett. A crowd had gathered around the general store in response to all the commotion that had been going on there, but even that group wasn't big enough to hide the six-foot-four Garrett.

Clint shrugged to himself and headed down the street toward the bank. Since most of the town's law seemed to be wrapped up with Drezdev, he figured he might as well check out on his own the other places that were being set up to be robbed. As far as he could tell, Drezdev didn't have a big enough gang to be too concerned about and he might just meet up with Garrett along the way.

There was still plenty that needed to be done in White Sands and if nobody else was in too big of a hurry to get it done, then Clint might as well do it himself.

TWENTY-THREE

Clint went back to the bank and found nobody there. Just like the last time he'd passed by, not only weren't there any robbers or lawmen, there was nobody there at all. Not even anybody passing by like they'd done less than an hour ago. Of course, a lot of that could be attributed to the fact that a growing amount of folks were still gathering around the general store, but Clint went up to the front of the bank anyway and peeked inside.

The place looked as though it had been deserted for years. Just to be sure, Clint walked around the building to look inside wherever he could. After a quick inspection, he decided that there wasn't anybody inside the place.

Clint thought back to the places he'd discussed with Garrett earlier. The only other one that the ex-lawman had talked about being scouted out by Drezdev was the saloon. Within the space of a few more minutes, Clint had jogged a few streets over and was approaching the Split Hitch Saloon. At first, the saloon looked just as deserted as the bank but when he got a little closer, Clint noticed that the front door was cracked open even though the sign in the window read CLOSED.

With his hand resting on the handle of his borrowed gun, Clint walked up to the front door and stood right next to it with his back pressed up tight against the wall. Using the tip of his boot, he nudged the door open just a little bit more so he could get a better look inside.

There was only one man that he could see inside the place. But, unlike the two he'd found inside the general store, this man seemed completely uninterested in looking for money or ransacking the saloon for any other valuables. This one stood alone, leaning against the bar, staring down intently at a glass.

Once Clint got a better look at the figure, he pushed open the door and walked inside. "Pat?" he said. "Is that you?"

The figure lifted the glass to his mouth and took a drink. When he turned around, Clint tensed a bit since he wasn't completely sure if he was right about the man's identity. But when the other man faced him head-on, Clint moved his hand away and started walking up to him.

"That is you, Pat. What are you doing here? Were there any more of Drezdev's men trying to rob this place too?"

"Nope," Garrett replied. "I just needed a drink. And since I was fairly sure there wouldn't be anybody else in here, this seemed like the best place to get one."

Clint walked up to stand next to Garrett. When he did, the ex-lawman leaned forward to reach beneath the bar and pull up an open bottle of whiskey. He set the bottle down with a solid *thump* and pushed it a little closer to Clint.

"Help yourself," Garrett said.

Clint walked around the bar and snatched a glass off the shelf behind the bar. "Actually," he said while pouring himself a beer from the nearby tap, "I'm not a big one for whiskey, but I could sure use a drink. We'll have to make it quick, though. Drezdev's hostages are being held in a barn outside of town."

"You can handle it just fine without me, Adams. I've heard a lot about you. This ain't nothing you can't handle. I'm not needed around here. All I need to do is crawl away somewhere and live out the rest of my days where I don't have to listen to people and they don't have to see my face. Maybe then I can go just one day without having somebody call me a back-shooting murderer."

Taking a few sips of his beer, Clint walked around the bar so that he was once again standing next to Garrett. Normally, he would think someone talking that way was just feeling sorry for himself. But, since most of what he'd heard about Garrett was pretty close to the "back-shooting murderer" line, he thought that Garrett might have good reason to feel a little down. Especially after risking his life to bring in another real killer only to get nothing but grief from the local law.

"How long will you be here?" Clint asked.

Garrett took another sip of his whiskey. "Long enough to greet Ben when he comes walking through that door to open this place back up for the night."

"Good. Just try to make sure he's got something left to serve to his customers."

Raising his glass in a silent toast, Garrett nodded once and turned his attention back to the top of the bar. He stared down with so much intensity that it appeared as though he'd found some kind of secret message written to him in the wood grain. Clint was uncomfortable leaving the hostages sit any longer, so he walked out of the saloon, hoping Garrett would be around when he came back.

TWENTY-FOUR

Finding the barn on the outskirts of town was not difficult at all. Even though Clint wasn't all that familiar with White Sands, he was aware enough to spot all the deputies riding in the general direction that Drezdev had mentioned. In a matter of minutes, Clint was able to get to the livery, saddle up Eclipse and race to the spot where the deputies had all gathered.

Sure enough, it was a secluded old barn with more holes than doors sitting like a dilapidated monolith on the edge of town. Clint swung down from Eclipse's back and strode inside, his hand resting over his gun just in case there were any surprises waiting for the lawmen inside.

The only thing waiting for him was a couple slope-backed cows and a trio of men bound and gagged at the back of a horse stall in the far corner of the building. Rather than stand away from the others, the sheriff was squatting down next to an older man, carefully removing the ropes from around his wrists and ankles.

Clint saw that most of the attention was focused on the two older men, while Ben had yet to be untied. Once he saw that the barkeep had spotted him, Clint made a show out of taking his time in getting to the big man's side. He tugged at Ben's

103

ropes and then finally pulled down the bandanna that had been tied around his mouth.

"Oh, so now you're trying to be funny, huh?" Ben said as he pulled the ropes completely off of him. "First these boys come in here and pretend they don't even see me and then you try to make a joke out of me almost gettin' killed."

"The crisis is over," Clint said as he offered his hand to help the barkeep to his feet. "Drezdev is in a jail cell right now."

"And what about Carlyle? He was the one itching to put a bullet in all of our heads."

"He's dead," Clint said simply.

Those two words seemed to take Ben by surprise. His head snapped back a little and then he looked around as though he half-expected to see Carlyle come charging into the barn with guns blazing. "Are you sure?"

"Yeah," Clint said. "I'm sure."

Still unnoticed by the deputies except for a few quick glances, Ben walked out of the stall and headed for the big, open door at the front of the barn. Clint followed him out, grateful to be away from the commotion and stench inside the old barn.

"So what did you ever do to those men in there?" Clint asked.

"What do you mean?"

"It looked to me as though they were taking their sweet time getting around to untying you. Hell, I might be hard-pressed to say if they weren't just going to leave you right where you were."

Ben smiled widely, displaying a mouthful of crooked teeth. Despite his appearance, however, the bartender possessed a certain charm, which made him one of those men that Clint instantly wanted to like. "I guess I'm just not rich or influential enough to merit any special treatment. Especially when the heads of business are the ones most responsible for getting that sorry excuse of a sheriff elected in the first place."

"So how long were they going to let you sit like that?"

"Aw, I wasn't too worried. They was bound to get thirsty sooner or later."

Ben leaned his head to one side and started rubbing at a sore spot on the side of his neck. It was the first time Clint had noticed the dark bruises covering a knot behind his ear the size of a strawberry. It was crusted over with blood and hurt Clint just to look at it.

"What happened there?" Clint asked, pointing to the wound.

"A little present from Carlyle. I told you he was the mean one of that group."

Ben then proceeded to tell Clint about what had happened from the moment he'd last left the saloon right up to when the deputies had found the barn. Clint listened and waited for any information that might let him know if he had anything else to worry about with Drezdev. As far as he could tell, the gang consisted of three people. One was dead. The other was in jail and the last was still nursing the wound Clint had given him at the Split Hitch.

Clint then told Ben about what Drezdev had been trying to do after kidnapping him and the other two businessmen.

"Well, you got to hand it to Drezdev," Ben said. "It might not be the most complex plan, but it wasn't exactly a bad one."

"True. But the only good plan is one you can walk away from with money in your pockets. Ending up in a cell with both your partners shot doesn't sound like a very good plan to me."

"I said it was a good *plan*, Adams. Drezdev and Carlyle, on the other hand, have their heads so far up their asses they have to bend over to scratch their noses."

As both men started laughing, the door to the barn swung open. Sheriff Pickering stepped out with his deputies and the two businessmen following closely behind. Almost immediately, the sheriff fixed Clint with a hard stare and a stern expression. Before he could say anything, he was bumped aside by the general store's owner, who rushed up to Clint and grabbed his hand.

"I just wanted to thank you, Mister Adams," the older man said. "Sheriff Pickering told me what you've done and I want you to know that you have my deepest and most sincere gratitude."

"That's much appreciated," Clint replied. "But I wasn't

alone. Pat Garrett helped me out. In fact, he saved my life."

The store owner stared at Clint as though he'd just been told that pigs had stood up on their hind legs, armed themselves and put a bullet through Carlyle's head. "Well . . . that's nice. I'll . . . certainly thank Mister Garrett the next time I see him."

"You be sure to do that."

The bank manager came by as well to offer Clint his thanks. And, just like the first hostage, he took on a dazed, somewhat distant expression when Clint mentioned that Pat Garrett had taken a part in their rescue. Besides seeing what could get under Garrett's skin with having to live among these kind of people, Clint started to wonder why the ex-lawman had risked his life at all for them.

Obviously, Garrett had an even stronger spirit than Clint had first thought.

After the deputies had ushered away the bank and store owners, Sheriff Pickering walked over to Clint. With a glance, he sent Ben away and said, "Shouldn't you be somewhere, Adams?"

"I tried the Split Hitch, but that didn't seem to be open for some reason."

"Then why not find another place to sit and drink? Anything to keep you busy while I try to do my job."

Clint fought back the impulse to vent some of the anger that had been building. Rather than let the sheriff know what he truly thought of him at that moment, Clint said, "Can I ask you a question?"

By way of a reply, the sheriff stared at Clint with his hands resting on his hips.

"What have you got against me?" Clint asked. "And while I'm at it, what have you got against Pat Garrett?"

"Personally, I don't have anything against Pat. My only problem with him is that he doesn't seem interested in taking his rightful place behind a badge. He's worked as everything from county sheriff to the Texas Rangers, but he won't work for me no matter how much I sweeten the deal."

"Can't say as I blame him. Why would anyone want to work somewhere he's not respected?"

"I'll be the first to give Pat his due. He just needs to own up to what he's done before he can be much good to anyone else."

Clint could hear the words coming out of the sheriff's mouth even before he said them. In fact, Clint wanted to divert the matter before any mention was made to Garrett shooting anyone in the back. "Then what about me?" Clint asked. "I've already been cleared of those charges. I've been set free legally by the judge in your own town. I've even helped you get these men to safety and stop Drezdev before he got out of town with his pockets full of money. He would've gotten away with his scheme if Pat and I hadn't stepped in. What was the problem anyway? Did those robberies interrupt your siesta?"

"Just because you've got that reputation of yours, don't think for one minute that I'll let myself be swayed into thinking you're some kind of savior," Pickering fumed. "You got damn lucky to have Judge Fountain on your side. Believe me, if it wasn't for him, this town would be a lot better off. Do you think that you're the first one he let go scott free just because of a feeling he had in his gut? When I see him act like that, it turns my stomach. So if you step out of line even so much as breaking our public intoxication laws, I'll toss your ass back into that cell and bury the key down your horse's throat. No judge in the world could save you if you just happen to get shot while I'm arresting you, Adams. You'd best not forget that."

Clint could feel his fists clenching and his teeth grinding together. Nothing made him angrier than a lawman who abused his power. And though he couldn't say if Pickering was exactly a crooked sheriff, he was most definitely one who thought he was bigger than the laws he'd been sworn to defend. Listening to such a man talk to him that way made Clint want nothing more than to bury his fist in the lawman's gut.

Sensing the anger that was boiling inside of Clint, Ben reached out to put a beefy hand on his shoulder. "It's been a long day for all of us," the barkeep said. "How about we all just settle down and have a drink?"

"Not while I'm on duty," Pickering said. "But you two go on ahead. In fact, charge Mister Adams's and Pat's drinks to my tab. It's the least I could do for all of their help."

Suddenly, Clint didn't care to watch the businessmen get escorted back to their homes. He didn't care what the sheriff or his deputies had in store for Drezdev and he certainly didn't care to waste any of his own time checking in on Krow. All he wanted was to wash his hands of this entire day.

TWENTY-FIVE

Standing at the bar in the Split Hitch, digging into a thick cut of steak and the next in his endless line of beers, Clint was really starting to appreciate Sheriff Pickering's generosity. What made it even better was that he doubted very much the lawman knew just how generous he was being.

"How you two doing over there?" Ben asked as he walked over to stand in front of Clint.

Pat Garrett was also there, but since he'd hardly said a dozen words in the last couple of hours, he might as well have been a tall piece of furniture attached to the bar by the elbows. He, too, was digging into a steak dinner, which was giving his system something else to run on besides whiskey.

Swallowing a mouthful of tender beef washed down with a sip of beer, Clint nodded at the barkeep with genuine satisfaction in his eyes. "Couldn't be better," he said. "In fact, I'd like to propose a toast." Raising his glass, he announced, "To Sheriff Pickering. The kind-hearted benefactor of this wonderful feast."

"And it's not over yet," Ben said with a wink. "The sheriff told me to treat you to whatever you'd like for this one visit. So as long as you don't walk out of here, keep right on feasting. It's the least I can do for someone who was content to let me sit tied up like a prize calf while he sets all the richer folks free."

The sound started out as a low grumble. Then, it built to a deep-throated chuckle that shook Garrett's shoulders and surprised the hell out of both Clint and Ben.

"What do you know?" Clint said in amusement. "The dead have arisen. What's the occasion, Pat?"

Once he was able to control his laughter, Garrett said, "I was just thinking about the look that's gonna be on Pickering's face when he sees this bill."

"And he *will* be seeing it," Ben said. "And he *will* be paying it."

For the next few moments, the three men at the bar joked around as though the events of the last twelve hours hadn't even taken place. They were too busy eating and swapping stories to think about the kidnapping and shooting that had nearly put an end to each one of them. But most importantly, Clint could tell that Garrett was thinking about other matters besides the ones that had weighed so heavily upon his soul.

After topping off Clint's and Garrett's drinks, Ben wiped off the top of the bar and started walking away. "As much as I'd like to stay and chat with you two gentlemen, I've got a business to run. Either one of you needs anything, just help yerself."

Clint took a look around and felt as though he'd fallen asleep for the better part of a day. It wasn't due to any effect of the beer he'd been drinking. It was more due to the fact that the saloon seemed to have filled up to the rafters in the time it had taken him to finish the last several bites of his steak. In that time, the piano player had started belting out his string of lively tunes and the showgirls had come out from the back to circulate among the crowd.

At that moment, Clint felt a soft, gloved hand settle onto his shoulder. The scent of rose petals and the slightest hint of perfume drifted into Clint's senses, followed by the light touch of Alison's hair on the back of his neck.

"Glad to see you're still in one piece," she whispered into Clint's ear. When she spoke, her lips glanced delicately over his skin.

Clint turned around and saw her standing there, wrapped in

a dark green dress that clung to her body and accentuated everything from the firm roundness of her breasts, the gentle slope of her hips, all the way down to the fine contours of her legs. She slid her hands around his neck to pull him in for a long, passionate kiss.

When he was finally able to pull himself away, Clint took a deep breath and tried to shake some of his senses back into his head. Once the fog cleared, he smiled widely and took Alison in his arms. "I'm still in one piece, all right. Did you expect any different?"

"Well, it's hard to say, especially since the last time I heard about you, you two were shooting it out with Drezdev. And the last time I saw you," she said, while pressing a finger against Clint's shoulder, "you were in a jail cell."

"I've actually got a lot of fond memories about that cell," Clint said.

Alison smiled warmly and ran both hands down his chest. "I'll bet you do."

Shaking his head while taking a sip from his drink, Garrett said, "I don't even want to ask about what you're talking about. Something tells me I'm better off not knowing."

"That's good, Pat," Alison chimed in. "Because a true lady wouldn't tell you anything even if you had asked."

Garrett made sure to step back out of arm's reach before saying, "Hey Clint, next time you see a lady, be sure and let me know."

Alison leaned forward so she could take a swing at Garrett and clipped the other man with the edge of her knuckles. The ex-lawman gave them both an off-handed wave before heading for one of the card tables toward the back of the saloon. Clint watched him leave and scanned the room. Suddenly, he picked out a familiar face in the crowd.

"What's Kieffer doing here?" he asked.

Alison was pressed up against him, running her hands down his back. "Same as always, I'd expect. Playing cards. Don't you have something a little more . . . urgent to think about right now?"

Clint was just about to follow Garrett over to Kieffer's table so he could ask the older man some questions about the shootings that had happened the other day when something kept him rooted to his spot. That something was Alison's probing fingers that had moved down his back, around to his front, and come to a rest directly on his crotch.

Smiling wickedly at him, she massaged the bulge in his pants and moaned under her breath when she felt him grow harder.

"Are you trying to distract me?" Clint asked.

"Only since the moment I saw you. And after the time you showed me in that cell of yours, I haven't been able to think about anything besides feeling your body on top of mine. I want to wrap my legs around you and feel you slip inside me so bad that I can taste it." Closing her eyes, Alison leaned her head back and ran her tongue slowly over her upper lip. "Mmmm. Yes, I can still taste it."

Now, Clint allowed his own hands to roam a bit over the contours of her body. He put his hand on her waist and pulled her in close until he could feel the warmth between her legs against his thigh. "Are you suggesting I try to land myself in jail again?"

"As much fun as that was, I was thinking of something a bit more traditional." Alison placed her lips against Clint's ear and flicked her tongue out to send a little shudder down his spine. "I've got a room upstairs. If you don't take me there quickly, I'm about to lose control of myself right here and now."

Clint was about to say something else, but Alison took hold of his hand, pulled him away from the bar and led him toward the back of the saloon where there was a narrow set of stairs leading to the second floor.

"Won't you be late for your next show?" Clint asked.

"That depends on how long you can last, cowboy."

"In that case," he said once they made it to the top of the stairs. "You might as well forget about the stage. You'll be doing all your dancing for me tonight."

Alison's smile grew to twice its size as she opened a door at the end of the hall and pulled him inside.

TWENTY-SIX

Alison's room was slightly bigger than the one at Clint's hotel. It had a small table and chair in one corner and a nightstand set up beneath a rectangular window that ran from the floor all the way up to the ceiling. Most of the space in the room was taken up by a large four-post bed covered with a thick cotton quilt. Alison let go of Clint's hand just long enough to pull the top of her dress down around her waist and then wriggle her hips so that the garment fell to the floor. Running her fingers through her hair, she let her chestnut-colored mane drape over her shoulders, the ends lightly brushing along the slope of her breasts.

Clint took in the sight of her standing naked before him, wearing only her high heels. Her lips were parted slightly. When she started walking toward him, her breath caused her breasts to heave slightly. Her nipples were already hard, pink little nubs.

Alison's hands worked quickly at his clothing, tugging it off piece by piece until she could run the palms of her hands over his naked body. Her eyes followed the path of her fingers as they circled his stomach and then began stroking his hard cock. After letting her massage him for a few seconds, Clint put his hands on her shoulders and then ran them down her back. Al-

113

ison's naked skin felt smoother than silk and when he began
kneading the muscles in her lower back, she rested her head
on his shoulder and began making a sound that could only be
compared to a purr.

As they continued their writhing dance against one another,
Clint and Alison had been working their way toward the bed.
Finally, the back of her legs bumped against the bed's frame
and she crawled up onto the mattress so that she was kneeling
on it facing him.

Clint brushed her hair back away from her face, savoring the
feel of her skin mingling with the soft, wispy strands. Reaching
down, he cupped her breasts with both hands and squeezed her
nipples just enough to make her take a breath in a quick, excited
gasp.

Alison laid down on her side, reaching out with one hand to
guide Clint's penis to her mouth. Opening her ruby-painted lips,
she extended her tongue so that she could swirl its tip around
the head of his cock before licking down along its shaft. Then
her lips closed around him and she started sucking on him. Her
head moved back and forth and her tongue danced inside her
mouth. When she started pulling back, Clint reflexively put his
hand behind her head so that the pleasure wouldn't come to an
end. In response to his insistence, she started purring again.
Only this time, with him inside her mouth, the vibration of her
voice intensified his pleasure even more.

Now a different type of urgency filled Clint's body. And
rather than give in to the approaching climax, Clint moved
away from Alison and crawled onto the bed next to her.

"What's the matter?" she asked with a sexy pout. "I thought
you liked it when I sang for you."

"It's time for my performance."

Clint's hands were already easing over her body. He brushed
over her breasts and slid down the smooth contour of her stomach until he could feel the downy thatch of hair between her
legs. Moving his fingers gently back and forth, he felt the moist,
delicate lips of her vagina, which spread open beneath his touch
as she began squirming slowly on the bed.

Sliding his finger inside of her and then slipping it back out,
Clint studied the way her body responded to his touch. When

he slipped two fingers inside, she smiled and tossed her head to one side. As he used his other hand to massage her breasts, she reached up over her head and grabbed hold of a pillow. And when he used his fingers to rub her own juices over her clit, she arched her back and started groaning loudly.

"Oh God, Clint," she moaned. "I want you inside of me." Her hands came down to tug at his shoulders, but her grip weakened as he once again slipped his fingers inside.

"I'm not through with you," he said. "In fact, you're going to do things my way."

Even though she twisted her face into a disappointed pout, Alison couldn't hide the fact that she was loving every bit of what Clint was doing. "But I want you now," she said as she started to sit up.

Clint put one hand on her and pushed her right back down to the bed. Landing with a soft *thump* against the mattress, Alison looked up at him with wide eyes that were charged with excited energy. She spread her legs open and reached down to take hold of his cock, lifting her hips so that she could feel it slide inside her pussy.

"I can't wait," she insisted. "I need you *now*."

It took every bit of willpower Clint had to keep from burying himself all the way inside of her. She managed to wrap one leg around his waist and was pulling herself toward him. Clint still got free and held her down with both hands.

"You want me to stop?" he asked as he lowered himself down. "You want me to crawl up on top of you instead of doing this?"

Alison stopped squirming as he moved his head between her legs and ran his tongue along the insides of her thighs. She tried to speak but couldn't get anything out besides a contented moan as he tasted her skin and licked the tender skin of her most sensitive areas. Her breath caught in her throat as he opened his mouth and placed his lips directly onto her vagina, sliding his tongue deep inside of her. Alison dug her fingers through his hair and started bucking against his face as the sensations swept like wildfire through every muscle in her body. When she felt like she was about to cry out, she turned her face into the closest pillow just as the tingling fingers of her orgasm ran through her skin and tickled every one of her nerves at the same time.

Clint could feel her muscles twitching. He kept his tongue inside of her even as her hips bucked and squirmed beneath him. Once she became still, he moved on top of her and grabbed hold of her hips. "You still want to dance?" he asked.

Alison responded by reaching down to once again stroke his cock. He was already rock-hard, so she wrapped her legs around him and fit him inside of her. Groaning loudly as he plunged his penis all the way inside, Alison threw her hands over her head and grabbed hold of the headboard as Clint began thrusting with a strong, steady rhythm.

Keeping his body upright, Clint kept hold of her hips as he pumped his cock between her thighs. He savored the way her buttocks clenched with every thrust and the way her body curved like a bow that had been bent toward his chest. Her breasts swayed gently as he pounded into her, the hard nipples looking like pink pieces of candy. Clint leaned forward so he could feel those nipples brushing against his lips and when he pinched them between his teeth, Alison cried out with pleasure.

Now it was her turn to pull away, but she only moved so that he was on his knees and she could switch positions beneath him. After sliding one leg between his, Alison got onto her side and put her other leg over Clint's shoulder. He slid back inside of her, grabbing hold of the leg that was pressed against his chest and pounding even deeper than he could before.

Once again, Alison was holding onto the headboard, but shifted around so that she could look back at Clint as he grunted and thrust himself inside of her until their bodies were pressed together as one. Watching him move as he made love to her, Alison slid her hands over her own body, pinching her nipples or even rubbing against Clint's shaft as it slid in and out of her.

Clint could feel the muscles in her vagina tightening around him. The sensation was so intense that his own climax started raging up to the surface until waves of pleasure swept through him, making him forget about everything else but himself and Alison. She, too, started moaning loudly with each thrust until they both cried out in a final explosion of ecstasy.

After his head stopped spinning, Clint felt as though he'd lost all of the strength required to keep him from falling over. He opened his eyes and looked down at Alison, who lay stretched out beneath him, her body still shuddering as the last remnants of her orgasm worked through her system.

Clint watched her body writhe and her smile grow wider until she finally let out the breath she'd been holding and ran her fingers through her hair. Opening her eyes, she looked up at him and sat up so she could wrap her arms around his neck. Alison planted a kiss on him that would've knocked him out of his boots if he'd been wearing any at the time.

She pulled him down so that she could lay curled up at his side with her head resting on Clint's shoulder. Tracing her fingertips through the hair on his chest, she said, "I still might be able to make it to the stage in time for the next show. That is . . . if you don't mind waiting up here for me."

"Did you think I was kidding when I said you'd miss your shows?" he asked. "I'm not good at working on someone else's schedule, so since I'm a free man again, you'll have to do what I say."

Her eyes widened and she moved so that she was laying on top of him. She straddled his hips and started rubbing herself up and down against his sweaty body. "I guess I'm at your mercy, then," she whispered.

Already, Clint could feel his penis getting harder as Alison squirmed on top of him. In a matter of seconds, he was inside of her and pumping his hips slowly up and down. Alison smiled luxuriously and leaned back to enjoy her ride.

TWENTY-SEVEN

Having just finished up another workout with Alison, Clint was just about ready to get an hour or two of sleep when he heard the sound of footsteps pounding up the stairs. The steps were so heavy that if anything had been hanging on the walls, it would have surely fallen off and shattered on the floor. Clint's first reaction was to go for his gun, which caused Alison to awake with a start since she'd been curled up right next to him.

"Clint, what's wrong?" she asked as she wiped away the sleep from her eyes.

Clint didn't say a word; instead, he got his gun and turned to face the door just as the footsteps came thundering down the hall. It took him a moment to adjust his aim since the weight of Garrett's pistol was slightly different than his familiar Colt. There was just enough time, however, for him to snap back the hammer and snatch one of the blankets from the bed, which he used to wrap around himself before heading for the door.

Seeing Clint's reaction and then hearing the approaching steps, Alison wrapped the sheets around her and drew her knees up tightly toward her chest. A trace of fear trickled into her voice when she said, "Clint, tell me what's going on."

"There's someone coming in a big hurry out there."

The footsteps had slowed down a bit, but they were still

drawing closer. Clint could almost picture whoever it was taking a moment to draw a weapon while studying each door in turn.

"Maybe they're looking for someone else," Alison suggested in a whisper.

Clint shook his head. "It's never that easy. Besides, I'd rather be safe than—"

He stopped at the same time as the footsteps came to a halt. Whoever steps they were, they'd stopped directly outside of Alison's door. Clint reached out and took hold of Alison's hand. After pulling her down so that she was on the floor with the bed positioned between herself and the door, Clint got to his feet and listened as the steps shuffled outside.

The door's knob rattled slightly, so Clint took aim, preparing himself to shift the pistol the moment he saw his target.

Suddenly, the doorknob stopped moving. After years of experience, Clint got the most nervous when things got too quiet, so he crouched down slightly and put all of his senses on full alert. When the person outside started pounding on the door, it sounded like a hammer smacking against the flimsy wood.

"Mister Adams?" came a muffled voice from the other side of the door. "Mister Adams, are you in there?"

Clint thought he recognized the voice, but couldn't quite put a face to the sound. After making sure Alison was hidden beneath the bed, he moved away from the door so that he wouldn't be in the line of fire if someone decided to start shooting into the room from the hallway. "Yeah?" he said cautiously. "Who is it?"

"It's James McDonnell. I'm one of Sheriff Pickering's deputies."

Still cautious, Clint stepped a little closer to the door, but was ready to jump in any direction if something happened. "What do you want?"

"You need to come with me, sir."

Suddenly, Clint felt his anger boiling up again. Just the thought of being chucked into a cell again for no good reason made him want to wrap his hands around Pickering's throat and shake some sense into that thick skull of his. He wasn't, however, mad enough to forget about why he'd been so careful up to this point. Rather than storm outside, he threw off his blanket and quickly got into his pants and shirt.

With his hair a rumpled nest on top of his head and his clothes hastily tossed over his body, Clint snatched the gun back into his hand and approached the door. It had only taken him less than a minute to get dressed, but that was more than enough time for the deputy outside to start getting restless.

"Mister Adams?" said the muffled voice. "You really need to—"

When Clint opened the door, he kept his gun out of sight so as not to spook the man on the other side without reason. The door only came open a crack, giving Clint a narrow view of the deputy's surprised face. As far as Clint could tell, Mc-Donnell was alone. But he wasn't about to bet his life on that.

"I need to what?" Clint asked.

"If you could just come with me, there's been a problem and—"

"I've been here the whole night," Clint said, his hackles rising. "Whatever Pickering thinks I did, you can just tell him I couldn't have done it. If you need witnesses, just ask Ben downstairs, or Garrett. They'll tell you I haven't left this place since I got here hours ago!"

"But that's just it. Mister Garrett is the one who sent me up here for you."

Clint felt as though he'd been hit from a blind spot. Of all the things he'd been expecting up to this point, that hadn't been one of them. He studied the nervous features of the kid on the other side of the door and opened it a little farther. Glancing left and right to make sure there was nobody else around, Clint looked back at the deputy.

"Mister Garrett said you wouldn't want to be bothered since you had . . . uh . . . company." With that last word, Mc-Donnell's eyes flicked over Clint's shoulder as though he knew exactly who was sharing the room with him. "That's why he just sent me up here."

"Why didn't he come himself?"

"Because he had to rush over to Judge Fountain's place. That's where the sheriff is, too."

Clint sighed heavily and lowered his gun. "If I have to go to trial after all, I'll be there in the morning."

"No, sir. It's Judge Fountain. He's missing."

That brought Clint out of his anger and threw him into an entirely different state of mind. "What? Missing?" He threw open the door and started to charge out into the hall before he realized that he wasn't fully dressed and wasn't even wearing any boots. "Give me a minute," Clint said to the deputy. "I'll be right there."

Clint stepped back inside the room and shut the door. When he turned around, he saw Alison standing with her sheets wrapped loosely around her body, watching him with wide, frightened eyes.

"What's wrong?" she asked.

Clint was already sitting on the edge of the bed, pulling on his boots. "Something's happened to Judge Fountain. The deputy outside says he's missing."

"Oh my God."

"It must be pretty bad since Garrett went through all the trouble of sending for me."

"But, why is he bothering with this? Isn't that the sheriff's job?" Alison sat next to Clint and quickly buttoned his shirt. "Pat never even got along with Sheriff Pickering, so why would he help him? Why would the sheriff even need his help?"

Clint stood up and tried not to let himself get overwhelmed by Alison's constant barrage of questions. What made everything worse was the fact that every word she said was drifting through his own mind as well. Hearing them come from her only made him feel as though his thoughts were echoing about the room and bouncing back into his ears from every angle.

"Look," he said once he was dressed and ready to go. "I don't know what's going on, but I'm set to find out. Judge Fountain is a good man and I owe him my freedom. If something's happened to him, I'll do my best to help."

"Just be careful, Clint. I've got a bad feeling about all of this."

"Yeah," Clint said as he walked toward the door. "So do I."

TWENTY-EIGHT

Once they got outside, the deputy quickened his steps until Clint had to jog to keep up with him. He'd lost track of time after dozing off next to Alison and the sky was colored with the thick, ominous black of the hours too early to be considered morning and too late to be considered night.

"What time is it, anyway?" Clint asked.

McDonnell didn't even look up. He had his eyes fixed on a spot directly in front of him as though that was the only thing keeping him going in a straight line. "It's a bit past three in the morning. The sheriff and Mister Garrett have been at the judge's for over an hour now."

The pair walked through the night without another word passing between them. Clint had no clue as to where the judge lived, but he could hear a group of voices no more than a block away. He figured that was where they must be headed since the rest of the entire town seemed to be asleep. They turned a corner to find about a dozen people milling about on the street outside of a house at the end of the block.

"Right there, Mister Adams," the deputy said, although Clint had already jogged ahead. When the younger man saw that he wasn't talking to anyone but himself, he hurried up to meet the rest.

123

It was hard to see much through the small crowd that had gathered outside the large house, but once Clint got a little closer, he was able to make out the faces of a few of the by-standers. Since none of them were the people he was looking for, Clint shoved his way through the group to get a look at the house itself.

The first thing he saw was the mess of glass that lay scattered on the dirt in front of the picture window. Looking inside through the empty frame, Clint was instantly reminded of the storefront where he and Garrett had confronted Drezdev and Carlyle what felt like so long ago. Like that scene from earlier in the day, the house in front of him now was a broken shell riddled with splintered wood, drops of blood and bullet holes. The front door swung lazily back and forth on its one remaining hinge, giving Clint an occasional glimpse of two men standing just inside the threshold.

One of the men, as though sensing Clint's presence, turned around sharply and pushed the door open all the way. "Clint, thanks for showing up," Garrett said as he held the door in place. "Come on in here."

Clint stepped inside and took a long look around. The place looked as if the entire building had been picked up by a giant, shaken up like a piggy bank and then set back down roughly upon its foundation. There wasn't a single surface he could see that hadn't been swept clean, its contents dashed mercilessly to the floor. A small rocking chair stood by itself in one corner. And although it wasn't as plain to see in the dim light, another thing that caught Clint's eye was the pools of blood that had collected here and there on carpeting or in a corner.

"What the hell happened here?" Clint asked.

Sheriff Pickering stepped up and shot Clint his usual dis-dainful glare. After letting out an uncomfortable breath, he hooked his thumbs in his gun belt and said, "That's what we're trying to find out. Someone came and got one of my deputies while I was making my rounds. They said they heard gunshots and thought someone was robbing this place. I came by about that time and have been trying to find anything that might help me get to the bottom of this mess."

Clint could tell that the sheriff still didn't like the look of him, but was doing his best to tolerate his presence. "Have you talked to any of those people outside?"

"They're not much help," the sheriff grunted. "All they heard was gunshots and all they saw was a couple men charging out of here like their asses were on fire."

"What men did they see?"

"They didn't see any faces." This time, it was Garrett who answered. "A couple of them have some stories to tell, but you'll get the same amount of different tales as the amount of folks you talk to." Turning to Pickering, Garrett said, "If you'd excuse me for a second, Sheriff." And without waiting for a reply, Garrett escorted Clint back out through the door and into the street.

Once they were far enough away from the crowd to talk privately, Clint took one more look at Fountain's house and then turned to Garrett. "Please tell me you're going to fill me in on what I'm doing here."

"I've heard plenty of good things about you from plenty of people whose word I trust," Garrett said. "Hell, we've even been under fire together so I already know for a fact that I'd rather have you covering me than even the sheriff."

Garrett turned so that he was sure his back was to Pickering and his deputies. "This is a helluva mess we got here."

"A blind man could've told me that much."

"Right. And that same blind man could tell you that whoever we're dealing with doesn't give a damn for human life or even his own life if he's willing to go this far against someone like Judge Fountain."

"That still doesn't tell me why I'm here," Clint said.

"You're here because, if Fountain is alive at all, he won't be for very much longer. I've been through that house myself and can't find a trace of him or his son."

"Son? Judge Fountain has a son?"

"Yes," Garrett said gravely. "And he's the judge's pride and joy. Whoever did this is after something from the judge, otherwise they would've just killed him outright. My guess is that they took the boy to use against Judge Fountain to make the whole deal go through that much quicker. I need someone who works fast and works well. That is why I sent for you."

"And what if Fountain is already dead?"

Garrett's expression didn't change in the slightest. It was clear that even that grim possibility had already occurred to him more than once. "If that's the case, then I need someone who's got tracking experience and knows how to handle a killer once he's been cornered. When we do find this man, something tells me he's gonna be desperate. Although Sheriff Pickering might do alright, I don't want to jeopardize the lives of them young deputies."

Suddenly, Clint realized he'd still been thinking about Pat Garrett as a lawman. Indeed, it had been the man himself who'd reminded him otherwise. There was just something about Garrett that had changed since the last time Clint had seen him. Standing there in the middle of a crime scene, dealing with Pickering and the deputies, Garrett exuded a strong sense of confidence and authority. Even the sheriff seemed to defer to him.

"I don't mean to be out of line here," Clint said. "But if I'm going to help out on this case, shouldn't I be talking to the sheriff?"

"You'll talk to the sheriff in the morning. What I need from you right now is your word that you'll be with me for this one. It may be dangerous, but I believe you're the only man I can count on around here who will be of some use to me without getting himself killed in the process. If you don't want any part of it, trust me, I'll understand. But if you decide to help out, there's going to be a reward coming for the man who brings in whoever did this. Since Judge Fountain was well liked in his circles, I'm sure that reward won't be anything to sneeze at. Plus, I'll see to it that you're paid a salary for acting as a deputized assistant to the sheriff."

Clint felt slightly overwhelmed after hearing all of that at once. He'd gone from sleeping peacefully in the arms of a beautiful showgirl to standing at the scene of a kidnapping and possible murder in the space of half an hour. He shook his head and focused in on Garrett in an attempt to block out everything else that was going on around him.

"Wait a minute," Clint said. "I'd be one of Pickering's deputies?"

"He's the town law. You'd be working for the sheriff of Dona Ana County."

Suddenly, everything started to make just a bit more sense. "Don't tell me," Clint said. "Let me guess."

Garrett nodded. Pointing over to the crowd, he said, "You see that man over there? The one wearing the long coat over his nightshirt? He's not only a good friend of Judge Fountain, but he's also a senator for the state of New Mexico. And on top of all that, he thinks Sheriff Pickering isn't good for much more than breaking up bar fights."

"Even that's giving him a bit too much credit," Clint said.

"Well, the only thing keeping him from appointing me into the position of county sheriff is the fact that he doesn't have a Bible on hand to swear me in. But that'll get squared away tomorrow morning and after he appoints the new sheriff, you're as good as deputized."

Clint's hesitation was only because it had been a long time since he'd worn a badge, and he tried to avoid it.

"Judge Fountain was a value to this town and a family man besides," Garrett said. "I can't stand by and let some asshole drag him out of his own home like this. If we let this happen to a good judge, we might as well just throw our laws right out the window. The bottom line is that I could really use your help, Adams. But I won't force you into anything you don't want to do."

"There's just one thing," Clint said.

"Name it."

"I'm going to need my own gun back."

TWENTY-NINE

At first glance, the scene at Judge Fountain's house was one of total and complete chaos. Now that Clint knew he was going to be an official part of the investigation, he turned to look at the house and those around it with a new set of eyes. Ignoring the confused glances he was getting from the deputies, Clint walked to the front of the house and squatted down to get a better look at the ground just below the window.

"I can send for some more lanterns," Garrett said. "But it might be a better idea to wait until first light before straining your eyes in this dark."

Although the sun was still wedged deeply below the horizon, there was still a bit of illumination leaking out from the gaslights lining the street as well as from the lantern inside the house itself. Clint stared down at the ground after his eyes had adjusted to the shadows. "Don't bother," he said. "If there were any tracks around here, they were wiped out by the stampede that has already walked over this spot in the last couple hours."

Garrett stood in the doorway, running his fingers along the frame and inspecting a set of gouges that had been dug out of the wood. First, he felt the part of the frame facing the street, and then he touched the interior edge. "Just what I thought. Whoever shot this door did it from the inside."

"I think I might have found something, myself."

Leaning outside, Garrett said, "That was quick. I knew I'd rousted you away from that pretty gal of yours for a reason."

Clint's face twisted into a pained grimace. "Don't remind me."

"My apologies," Garrett said with a chuckle. "What did you find?"

Leaning down with his hands resting on the side of the house for support, Clint lowered his head to about a foot away from the ground and blew gently onto the dirt. "The tracks here are a big mess of more people than I can count, but there's one set that stands out from the rest."

Garrett walked over to Clint and crouched down next to him. At first, he couldn't see much of anything besides the glass-and dirt-covered ground. But once his eyes had adjusted, more details began making themselves known to him. Clint blew one more time, which took away a fine layer of dirt that had settled on the solidly packed ground.

"You see that?" Clint asked after he'd scooted back a couple inches.

Squinting as he got a little closer, Garrett was about to say no, but then he spotted a certain shape amid the layers of dirt. "You mean those two footprints?"

"That's it. Those two prints can still be seen under all the prints that have trampled over the area. And they're deeper, so that means that either the one who left them was awful big or . . ."

"Or he jumped out the window and landed in that spot," Garrett finished.

"You got it."

The newest sheriff of Dona Ana County straightened up to his full height and shook his head in admiration. "Only on the job for a few minutes and you're already trying to impress the boss, huh?"

Clint stood up as well, grunting slightly as the knots in his muscles worked themselves out the hard way. "Not really. Those are the only two prints that didn't get wiped out in the shuffle. We might be able to pick up where they lead in the morning, but I wouldn't put too much faith in that."

"At least we're further than where we started. Now we know that at least one of the killers came out through the window. That might even be what broke all that glass in the first place."

Looking intently at the bottom of the window frame, Clint felt carefully around the sill. "This really isn't that high off the ground. Maybe only two or three feet. Even someone your size wouldn't leave tracks that deep if they jumped. Not unless they were carrying something heavy."

"Or someone."

"How old was Fountain's son?"

"I'm not sure. Seven or eight, maybe."

"Small enough to be slung over someone's shoulder?"

"He wasn't a small kid, but he'd fit over someone's shoulder easily enough. If you take into account that he was probably kicking and squirming the whole way, I'd say the man who took him had to be pretty big, himself."

"Oh, he was big all right," Clint said, glancing back down at the footprints. "And we can only hope the kid was still well enough to squirm when he was being taken."

Just then, the front door slammed open and Sheriff Pickering came storming out. Even though Clint had never seen the man look happy, he looked even more angered than usual. "So that's it, is it? You get the nod from some politician and you think you can waltz on in here and take over my job?"

"If the senator thought you were up to it," Garrett said without batting an eye, "I'm sure he would've told you."

"You ain't got the badge yet, Pat. So unless you want to spend your first day in office nursing a broken jaw, I'd suggest you stop trying to tell me my business."

Clint looked from one man to another, moving his eyes between Garrett and Pickering. The tension crackled in the air like an approaching storm, causing the hair on the back of Clint's arms to stand on end. The more seconds passed without a word coming from either man, the more Clint feared that something was going to snap inside one of the sheriffs.

Garrett let another second pass before he took a few slow, deliberate steps toward the sheriff. He came to a stop when he was toe to toe with Pickering and stared directly into the other man's eyes. "You know what's funny? The fact that you talk to me like I'm a dog until you need something done right around here. If I remember correctly, it was you that brought me down here in the middle of a perfectly good poker game and now you got the balls to talk to me like that?"

Even though Pickering wasn't making any sort of move toward Garrett, Clint moved his hand closer to the pistol at his side. It was a reflexive response to the raw anger that snapped between the other two like a spark.

"You feel threatened because in a few hours I'll outrank you?" Garrett asked. "Well maybe that's not a bad notion to have. Especially because if you ever talk to me like that again I'll put you on your ignorant ass, right in front of all your men, so the whole world can see just who belongs in the chase and who belongs behind a desk."

Pickering was fuming so badly that every one of his breaths sounded like steam escaping from a train's engine. His fists clenched and opened and then clenched again with such force that he could only have been imagining it was Garrett's neck inside his grasp instead of a whole lot of cold, empty air.

It took a while, but finally Pickering was able to step away from Garrett without taking a swing at him. He turned to walk inside the house, which was when he noticed that every one of his deputies were watching him with disbelief in their eyes. Pickering paused before stepping through the busted doorway and looked over his shoulder. "You watch yourself, Pat. These ain't punk kids we're after here. And they'll sure as hell know better than to turn their backs on you."

Pickering stepped inside the judge's house and gathered his deputies in a small circle around him. After talking to them for no more than half a minute or so, he stormed out of the building with his men following close behind. A few of the deputies looked back at Clint and Garrett, some obviously wanting to stay and others simply taken aback by all that had happened in one night.

Watching the deputies, Clint couldn't help but shake his head and laugh under his breath.

"Glad somebody thinks this is funny," Garrett said once Pickering and the others had cleared out.

"I just know how they feel, that's all," Clint replied.

THIRTY

Garrett stood in his regular spot at the bar inside the Split Hitch. Even though there were hardly any people inside the saloon and Ben was nowhere to be seen, at least the place was open. Clint walked straight through the front door and up to Garrett.

"Is it official?" Clint asked.

By way of response, Garrett turned and held open the right side of his coat to reveal the badge that was pinned to the front pocket of his dark gray shirt. Without a word, he tossed something through the air toward Clint and then turned to finish his drink.

Reflexively, Clint plucked the object from the air and held it in his fist. When he opened his fingers, the deputy badge winked at him with light reflected from the sun that streamed in through the front windows. With all the ceremony that he normally gave to getting dressed in the morning, Clint pinned the badge to the inside of his vest and signaled for the bartender.

"I'll take some coffee," Clint said.

Garrett waited until the drink came before saying, "You look ready to go. I take it you didn't see Alison after we parted ways."

Suddenly, Clint felt a pang of remorse for not having visited the showgirl since he was called away the night before. He didn't have any obligations to her, but then again he didn't want to use her up and then forget about her completely. "I was too tired to do much of anything but collapse."

"Well, I'm glad to see you took my advice. We got ourselves a long day ahead of us." Garrett was drinking from a metal cup, which he now lifted to his mouth and tipped all the way back. The smell of strong coffee drifted through the air as the brew ran through his system like a revelry. Fatigue from the night before showed on his face in the form of dark circles under his eyes and the slight bowing of his head. After that last drink, however, Garrett perked up somewhat and set the cup back onto the bar.

Clint realized firsthand how Garrett could awaken so quickly the moment he took a sip of his own coffee. The stuff was even worse that the coffee he'd had when he'd first gotten to town. It tasted like muddy tar and was almost too thick to be considered liquid. As soon as it hit his tongue, it seemed to take on a life of its own and run down his throat in a stampede of pure energy. "Damn," Clint said once he was able to draw a breath. "They should use this stuff to fuel trains. The Union Pacific would save a fortune on coal."

"I talked to Senator Avery after he swore me in," Garrett said, ignoring Clint's comment. "He said that this whole thing has to be cleared up as soon as possible because Judge Fountain was getting ready to rule on a dispute over one of the local cattle empires. It seems two local factions are vying for rights to the same area and if a decision doesn't get handed down soon, there'll be hell to pay."

"What kind of hell?"

"The kind that leads to war."

New Mexico was no stranger to wars between cattle barons. In fact, neither was Pat Garrett. After all, it had been the Lincoln County War between John Tunstall and L. G. Murphy that had changed a two-bit thug named William Bonney into the notorious killer Billy the Kid. And it was the Kid who'd brought Pat Garrett, for better or worse, into the position he was in at this very moment.

Clint was no admirer of the Kid, but he was also very familiar with how public perceptions could change the way a man's actions were viewed. Some thought of Billy as a hero, while others thought of him as a mad-dog killer. Those same people saw Pat Garrett as belonging in one of those two categories as well. And although Clint did his best to judge men based on what he knew of them firsthand, it was hard to look at Garrett and not see Billy's ghost lurking somewhere nearby.

Garrett's voice broke in on Clint's thoughts, bringing him back to the present situation. "I've also been talking to some of the folks that were there when the Fountains were attacked. They say they saw two men go in and two go out."

"That can't be," Clint said. "Otherwise, there would've been some bodies back at the house."

"Or some of them escaped without being seen. Of all the people I spoke to, only a few of them were actually outside when there was something to see and only one of that bunch got a look at one of the men's faces."

"Who was the man I shot when we were attacked here—Krow?"

Garrett nodded. "That's right, but the man I talked to said he saw someone shorter and with a little more meat on his bones than Krow. It sounded to me like Deacon Hobbs."

Clint thought for a second and then shook his head. "Can't say as that name rings any bells."

"Deacon's a killer for hire who's worked in the southwest for the last six years or so. He specializes in getting rid of people that most other outlaws won't touch for one reason or another."

"Like judges?"

"Yes, as well as lawmen or businessmen that are either too well protected or too much trouble to go after themselves. They hire Deacon to take these messy types of jobs so they don't have to be the one with the price on their head so big that every bounty hunter within five hundred miles will be after them. Deacon's good at staying out of sight. Hell, every other lawman you talk to says the man's dead already."

"That's the best cover to have."

"Which is exactly why I'm not one of those men who thinks he's dead. In fact, I know he's been around these parts lately and killing Fountain is the type of job that Deacon was born for. The only question now is who hired him."

THIRTY-ONE

Clint took another sip of his coffee. Now that his system was ready for the wallop it packed, the brew slid down a bit easier. "I still say we should check up on Krow. He's the only one of Drezdev's men we haven't accounted for since the robbery and just because he's wounded doesn't mean he's out of the picture."

"I agree. There's also another angle I want to check up on myself," Garrett said as he stared down at his empty cup. "I'll take care of that while you check on Krow."

There was something about the way Garrett was talking that didn't sit well with Clint. Perhaps it was something in his voice or even the way his eyes drifted down toward the bar when he spoke those last couple of sentences. Clint had been thinking of a particular angle himself which, if Garrett had known about, might have produced a very similar reaction.

Deciding that he would be of no use to Garrett unless he put all his cards on the table, Clint waited a second and said, "Are you talking about Pickering?"

Garrett's first reaction was to turn on Clint with a cold sharpness chiseled into his features. His eyes were steely slits and his mouth was set into a hard frown. But in the next second, the intensity faded away, only to be replaced by regret touched with the slightest hint of shame. "Yeah," he said quietly. "That's who I was talking about. What gave me away?"

"Nothing really," Clint said. "If anything, it was Pickering himself who made me suspect him. He didn't seem too happy with the judge's method of reading the law and he certainly didn't approve of how Fountain treated me. I got the impression that the sheriff was threatened by someone coming into his jail and telling him what to do."

"Most sheriffs would, Clint."

"True, but that doesn't seem like enough of a reason to do something as extreme as kidnapping him and his son."

"No," Garrett said with finality. "There's suspicion in both our minds, though, which means it's worth looking in to." It was obvious by the way he said it that Garrett was not happy about that part of the investigation, but was resigned to doing it anyway.

"Has anyone even heard from the kidnappers yet?" Clint asked.

"Nope. Not a word."

That was the answer that Clint had been least expecting and when he heard it, everything else was cast in a different light. "This just doesn't add up. If Fountain was kidnapped, then what are the kidnappers' demands? Why wait so long after they must know that they've got everyone's attention? And if these men wanted to kill Fountain, why take off with the bodies when they could've left a bigger message by leaving them out for all to see? I've been thinking about those tracks I found outside Fountain's house. It seems to make more sense that whoever jumped out that window was carrying the boy over his shoulders. Otherwise, the footprints wouldn't have been so evenly spaced." Holding his hands together to illustrate his point, Clint said, "They looked like someone jumped outside and landed on both feet. I don't think someone would try that with a full-grown man on his back."

Garrett looked over at Clint as though he was about to dismiss the line of reasoning, but then his eyes brightened and he looked down at Clint's hands as if he could actually see the outlines in the dirt. "So that means the judge was either already gone or still inside the house as his son was being taken away."

"That's right. You got a look at the door frame, right?"

"Sure did." Suddenly, Garrett snapped his fingers and slapped the palm of his hand flat against the bar. "The man that put those bullet holes in that frame did it from the inside. Judge Fountain didn't own a gun that I know of and if he did, he wasn't the type to shoot someone standing on his porch. I've seen him deal with killers worse than Drezdev without so much as blinking."

"And if the killers were already inside, why would they shoot the place up so badly when they should be more concerned about getting what they came for and getting out? If it is Deacon who pulled this off, it sounds to me like he would know a hell of a lot better than that."

"He would indeed." Energized by the sudden rush of ideas, Garrett paused for a few seconds to go over a couple of things in his own mind. His face brightened as though his sudden change of spirit was actually shining through his skin. After slapping enough money on the counter to cover both of their drinks, he motioned for Clint to follow as he headed for the front door.

Once they were in the open and away from most of the people standing along the sides of the street, Clint pulled Garrett aside. "I don't think that the kidnappers were the only ones doing the shooting inside that house."

"I'm beginning to think that same thing. Judge Fountain may not have been a fool, but he might have started shooting if he saw someone going near his boy. And with all those people standing outside when we got there, I have a hard time believing that only one of them saw anything worthwhile."

"How well liked was Fountain around here?" Clint asked.

"He did a lot of people a lot of good. He was one of the few that had kind words for me when I came here and that's saying a helluva lot." Taking a deep breath, Garrett nodded as though he'd finally gotten himself to come to terms with an unpleasant piece of fact. "I was thinking that some of those witnesses might not be telling me the whole story. But until now, I never had a reason of why they would lie to me. Unless they were covering up for someone."

"What I need to do is get back to that house so I can take a better look now that it's daylight and I have all my wits about me," Clint said. "Maybe I'll catch something we missed before."

"Better check in with Krow first. The sheriff wasn't too happy about being put on the shelf for this case and he'll only get more uncooperative as time goes by."

That brought Clint around to another point he'd been thinking about since he'd first been called to the Fountain home. "Has Pickering done anything in the past to make you think he might not be . . ."

Garrett stepped in to fill the pause in Clint's question. "If you're asking if I ever thought he was dishonest, then I don't have much of an answer for you. I've been a lawman for plenty of years and have seen good men turn into crooks after a lifetime of hard, honest work just because someone offered the right amount of money. Then again, I've seen men turn down a fortune for the sake of a job that barely pays to put food on their table. I couldn't tell you if Pickering is crooked or not, but I can say that he's capable of making a wrong turn. Hell," Garrett said as a familiar shadow crept over his face, "we're all capable of that."

Clint wanted to ask Garrett about what really happened on the last night Billy the Kid was alive. He'd been wanting to know ever since he'd come face to face with the man who'd shot him, but had never found the right time. Now was certainly not the right time, but the stories Clint had heard about Garrett kept coming back to nag at the back of his mind. After all, now that he was working for Garrett, it became more important to Clint to know what kind of man he truly was.

Settling on the fact that he would still have to wait to bring up what happened at Fort Sumner, Clint brought his mind back to more pressing matters. "Speaking of Sheriff Pickering, I still need to reclaim some of my property from him."

"Glad you reminded me," Garrett said. Opening his jacket, he reached for the left side of his gun belt where a pistol hung from a second holster at his hip. "It was my first act in my new office," he said while hefting Clint's modified Colt. Garrett placed it into Clint's waiting palm. "I wouldn't want you getting into another scrape with that old piece of steel I loaned you."

Clint handed over Garrett's pistol. Before he could ask about his own holster, Garrett had unfastened the belt that had been strapped around his waist, crossed over his own gun belt in a style preferred by some outlaws. The belt fit around Clint's waist as though he'd been born to wear it. The weight of his Colt balanced him out, making him feel completely himself again.

"That gun of yours wasn't bad," Clint said as he snapped through a few practice draws. "But it sure feels good to have things back to normal."

"Well . . . if Deacon is anywhere around here, you're gonna need that pistol quicker than you think."

THIRTY-TWO

Deacon Hobbs prided himself on two things above all others: his aim and his ability to hide. For most men, hiding wasn't exactly a thing to be proud of. But when Deacon thought of the word, he remembered all the times he'd walked into a town where he was wanted by the law as well as every bounty killer in the county and managed to conduct his business without being seen.

He didn't hide in a hole or cave somewhere like most outlaws on the run. Deacon lived his entire life on the run, which meant he'd taught himself to hide while walking around in plain sight. He knew just when to look away from someone's gaze and when to make himself so imposing that everyone else looked away from him. Once he'd mastered that, he'd become one of the best hired guns in New Mexico.

Deacon had been up since the break of dawn, watching the judge's house to see what the law was going to do about what had happened there. He wasn't too surprised to see Pat Garrett poking his nose around since he'd known Judge Fountain personally. Clint Adams, on the other hand, took Deacon by surprise.

Deacon didn't like surprises.

Surprises were one of those things that tended to get a man killed in a hurry.

Deacon was more used to being the surprise, which had been the single factor putting him at the top of his very deadly game.

When he'd seen Clint Adams, Deacon first thought the shadows were playing tricks on him. After all, what would the Gunsmith be doing poking around in the dirt at the scene of a shooting? Now that he'd had a chance to scout around White Sands after the shadows had been banished by the blazing sun, Deacon was certain that the man at Garrett's side was Clint Adams.

Deacon stood with his back against a post outside of a small restaurant across from the Split Hitch. He'd been there, waiting for Garrett to stick his face out, when Clint Adams had walked right by and into the saloon. Of course Adams hadn't spotted him there. Why would he? Dressed in worn jeans and a simple brown vest over a faded white shirt, Deacon wasn't exactly the type to stand out in a crowd. His dusty brown hair sprouted from a beaten old hat and hung down to just past his shoulders. Calm, steely eyes peered out at the world without revealing anything that went on behind them. They could have been the eyes of one hell of a poker player, but instead they belonged to a killer.

A killer whose only bluff was that he was just another unassuming bystander who wasn't ready to draw and put a bullet into anyone who was stupid enough to call him on it.

Deacon didn't bother thinking about what had happened the night before. Since that would have only angered him, he focused on what he needed to do at this moment and how he could make it all work out to his advantage.

While he was plotting silently, Deacon stood against his post, nodded to the folks that passed by and smiled politely whenever he received a word of greeting. Not one of the people who saw him thought much of anything about the stranger. And once something else caught their attention, most of them forgot about Deacon completely.

That was his gift. And it was that same gift that had gotten him into Judge Fountain's home the night before.

Deacon thought back to the previous night and tried to find

the source of what had gone wrong. It didn't take him long to arrive at his conclusion, since it had obviously been the fault of the man who'd hired him. If that man had kept his wits about him and not panicked as Deacon was making his escape, things would have turned out much differently.

The blood in Deacon's veins started pumping faster when he thought about the way things had happened. For a man who prided himself on his work, going through a botched job like that was a shot aimed directly at his soul. It burned him inside to have been a part of that. The only thing that made him feel better was that the man most responsible for the screw-up had gotten exactly what was coming to him. Not only that, but he'd gotten it in a way that diverted even more attention from Deacon Hobbs.

At that moment, the doors to the saloon had come open to allow Adams and Garrett to walk outside. Deacon's sharp eyes caught the glint of metal coming from just inside the edge of Adams's jacket, which he knew immediately to be a badge.

So, he thought, Garrett had found himself a deputy. Maybe sticking around White Sands wasn't such a good idea after all.

Deacon watched as the pair walked to the mouth of a nearby alley and took a step into the narrow space between buildings. They talked some more until Garrett handed a gun to Adams.

When Deacon saw that pistol, he had to fight back the urge to walk over and throw down on both men right then and there. He knew he hadn't been spotted yet, which would make it that much easier to end the career of the Gunsmith once and for all. But Deacon suppressed the impulse since that was something to be expected from any small-time shooter trying to make a name for himself.

Deacon had already made his name and if Garrett or Adams decided to interfere in his business, he would make sure they'd curse the day they'd ever heard it.

THIRTY-THREE

As Clint walked down the street on his way to the doctor's office, he couldn't shake the feeling that he was being followed. Although it wasn't very far from the saloon to the doctor's office, every step of the way found him wanting to look over his shoulder or question every glance that came his way. Clint pushed the feeling to the back of his head, knowing full well that it wouldn't go away for as long as he was tracking down the men who'd kidnapped Judge Fountain. The fact that he suspected the town's sheriff didn't help things, either.

Once he stepped inside the small office at the end of Main Street, Clint felt somewhat better simply because he had other things to occupy his thoughts. The first thing he did once he entered was scan the room for any trace of Will Krow. The doctor's office resembled a small house that had been hollowed out, leaving only two main rooms.

The front room took up most of the available space and was filled with a few cabinets and eight beds divided evenly into two rows. From where he was standing, Clint could see the smaller room in the back, which appeared to be a small office.

"Hello?" came a wavering voice that was tinged with an English accent. "I'll be with you in just a moment."

Only two of the beds were occupied and just as Clint was

about to take a look at the patients, he saw someone walking out of the back office. The doctor was dressed in black pants and white shirt with a long black coat. The front of his shirt had old-fashioned ruffles that reminded Clint of something he'd seen in a painting. The collar was stiff and buttoned all the way up to his chin, surrounded by a small black bow tie.

"Are you injured, sir?" the well-dressed man asked.

"Not at all. My name's Clint Adams and I'm here on official business."

Extending his hand, the man said, "I'm Doctor Hartnell. I don't believe I've seen you around here as of late."

The doctor's face was dominated by a large, hawkish nose and a wide, friendly mouth. His eyes bore the scars of his years around the edges, while also reflecting the wisdom gained in that time. Even though his scalp was bald until well past his ears, the doctor's thick snowy hair came all the way down to the middle of his neck.

Clint shook Dr. Hartnell's hand, which was as strong and steady as a rock that had spent its entire existence defying the push of a stream. "Actually, I've only been in town a few days."

"Well, that explains it, doesn't it. You mentioned something about official business?"

"I did, sir," Clint said as he opened his vest to display the badge pinned to its lining. He didn't usually wear a vest, but he'd put it on specifically so he could keep the badge hidden until he wanted to show it. "It's about a patient of yours named Will Krow. I'd like to speak to him."

"A few days in town and already a deputy?"

"I guess I'm qualified for the job. Now, about that patient of yours—"

"Sheriff Pickering approve of you?"

"Excuse me?"

"Sheriff Pickering," the doctor repeated. "Was he the one who approved of you becoming a deputy? I guess he would since he's the sheriff, but I find it hard to believe after knowing the man for . . ."

Clint stopped listening to what the old man was saying and started having a look around the office for himself. Dr. Hartnell's voice was a constant drone in his ears, but none of it made it all the way through to Clint's brain. He did notice, however, when the doctor stepped in front of him just as he was about to look in on one of the patients lying in bed.

"Can I help you with something?"

"Just the same thing as when I walked in here."

"Who exactly are you looking for? Perhaps I can tell you what you want to know before you start disturbing all of the people under my care."

"William Krow. I need to speak to him."

"Ahhh. Why didn't you just say so before?"

"I *did* say so be—" Clint stopped himself in mid-sentence, forced a friendly smile onto his face and started again. "He was brought in with a gunshot wound the other day and I need to talk to him."

"That's going to be rather difficult."

Clint had his eye on one of the patients in particular. He was lying on one side with his feet hanging over the foot of the bed. By the looks of him, the patient probably weighed less than the narrow wooden frame beneath him. "It's no bother at all," Clint said. "I'll just ask my questions and be on my way."

Dr. Hartnell rested his hand on Clint's shoulder. Although he didn't exert much force, he was strong enough to keep Clint from getting any closer to the bed he was headed for. "You can ask him whatever you want . . . when you manage to find him."

"What?" The word came out of Clint's mouth at the same time as he stepped free from Hartnell's grasp and walked around to the other side of the bed. The man lying there was the right body type and was indeed wounded. Unfortunately, he was most definitely not Will Krow.

Pulling Clint away from the stranger's bedside, Hartnell said, "Despite my misgivings, Mister Krow left this office yesterday. I bandaged him up and tended to him the best I could, but he refused to stay under my care. I advised against it, but it's not my place to hold people against their will."

"No," Clint growled as he thought about what he would do when he found Krow. "That's my job now."

THIRTY-FOUR

All the way to the doctor's office, Deacon could tell that Clint Adams was getting edgy. Every so often, Adams would look over his shoulder or stop and wait for someone to reveal that he'd been following him. He was looking for a suspicious face in the crowd, but he wasn't going to get it.

Deacon was too good to look suspicious. As far as anyone was concerned. Deacon had been born and raised in White Sands. Not even the locals paid him any mind.

He tailed Clint all the way to the doctor's office and picked a spot nearby where he could wait for him to come out again. Standing with his back against the side of a building in the cool shadows of an alleyway, Deacon watched the small office out of the corner of his eye while idly drumming his fingers against the wall.

When Clint did come out, he looked anything but happy. Deacon let him storm a ways down the street before falling into step behind him. The killer's steps were slow and easy. After all, he had all day to close this deal. Now that he'd been around Clint long enough to get a feel for him, he was confident in his ability to pick his moment and strike whenever the mood hit him.

It was almost going to be too easy.

• • •

At least the visit to Dr. Hartnell wasn't a complete waste of time. Before he'd left, Clint had asked a few more questions that actually might have been of some help. Apparently, even though Krow said he was going home when he'd left the doctor, Hartnell had a sneaking suspicion that he would be going to try and check in with his unsavory accomplices.

Just to make sure he was prepared for either possibility, Clint got the location of Krow's home as well as any other places he might try to meet up with his partners. Hartnell gave him the location of Drezdev's home as well. Since Clint knew that any other of Krow's partners were either dead or in jail, that left precious little places to check next.

He walked outside and took a breath of fresh air. It took a second or two to get his bearings, but he decided to check out the Fountains' home before anyplace else.

The uneasy feeling in the pit of Clint's stomach was back. This time, it gnawed at him relentlessly as soon as he left the doctor's office and started heading down the street toward Judge Fountain's house. He stopped looking over his shoulder since that didn't turn up anything on his way over. Obviously, if someone was following him, he was doing it well enough to keep from being spotted so easily.

And if nobody was following him, then Clint was just losing his mind from stress and lack of sleep.

Even though he hadn't found Krow at Hartnell's office, that didn't mean his visit to the doctor had been a waste of time. In fact, if Krow had been there, it would have meant that Clint's initial theory had been dead wrong. Now, confident in his conclusions, Clint knew he had to start looking for Krow if he was going to get any closer to finding the Fountain boy.

Of course Clint wanted to make sure that the judge was safe as well, but the more he thought about all that had happened, the less he thought that both of the missing Fountains were in the same place. He was hoping to find something to back that up at the judge's house and in the meantime, Clint was content to let whoever was following him keep doing so.

Just to make sure, Clint walked as though he didn't have a care in the world, right past the corner he'd been fixing to turn and straight up to the mouth of an alley two buildings over. He turned into the narrow passage and walked straight through to the other side. Once he emerged from between the two buildings, he quickly spun around and got ready to draw.

There was nobody in the alley yet, so he kept moving until he was standing with his back pressed up against a wall. Knowing that he would be out of the sight of anyone walking into or by the alley, Clint stood without making a noise, straining his ears for any sign that someone was coming after him.

He waited for a few seconds.

Nothing.

He waited just a bit longer and still there was not a sound.

Even as more time passed without hearing anything else besides the town's normal background noises, Clint was certain there was somebody out there with his sights on him. It was an instinct developed after decades of living on the edge of death where one misstep could spell the end to it all.

Once a man developed those instincts, he listened to them as though they were the voices of angels whispering in his ear. To ignore them was to throw away his desire to live since there were always those out there looking to put him into the ground.

Tired of waiting when there was nothing to hear or see from his current position, Clint took a quick glance around the corner and into the alley. Standing there, looking at him at the other end, was a man in plain clothes and a battered brown vest. As soon as Clint locked eyes with the other man, he knew that was the one who'd been following him.

Deacon wasn't about to follow Clint into an alley like some fool kid. Instead, when he saw Clint turn in between the buildings, Deacon had stopped at the edge of the alley and waited. He knew what Clint was about to do and he didn't want to be there when he took his first look over his shoulder.

Instead, Deacon waited a few seconds . . . letting his prey stew a bit before looking into his eyes.

At the count of ten, Deacon stepped into the mouth of the alley and waited there with his hands at his sides. From what he'd heard about the Gunsmith, he wouldn't draw first.

Deacon only had to wait another second before he saw

Adams's head pop around the corner. How easy it would have been to be waiting with his gun drawn and ready to put a bullet right through that skull of his. How anticlimactic for a legend like the great Clint Adams to get his brains blown out in an alley.

Although Deacon had bigger concerns than dramatic effect, he had other reasons for keeping Clint alive at the moment. And once those concerns were met . . . he could track his prey down one more time and finish him off.

Clint's eyes locked onto him from the opposite end of the alley. Putting on his best innocent, somewhat frightened look, Deacon lowered his head and walked away.

THIRTY-FIVE

By all appearances, Garrett wasn't doing a whole lot more than making a few social calls to friends in the area to announce his new appointment as county sheriff. He walked from door to door of various businesses and a few homes, saying hello to familiar faces and talking to them about all the various bits of gossip that had been floating around town lately.

Although each conversation was made to suit every individual person, Garrett was sure to steer things around eventually to include the disappearance of the Fountains. He still wasn't the most liked or even most trusted member of the community, but Garrett knew how to make himself more affable when in a position of authority. Folks always seemed to respond well to a lawman who didn't forget he wasn't better than anybody else. In fact, Sheriff Pickering might have had an easier time doing his job if he'd ever bothered to remember that simple fact.

Over the course of a couple hours, Garrett worked his way through Judge Fountain's neighborhood and even visited some of the witnesses at their places of work. Through all those conversations, he didn't get many more facts than he'd had before, but he did get something just as valuable: knowledge.

He knew, beyond all doubt, that those people were hiding

something from him. It wasn't a feeling or something as vague as a hunch. It was a plain and simple fact.

Mr. Wayne had been standing out in front of the Fountains' house even before Garrett had arrived there the night of the shooting. That man had been so panicked by what he'd seen that his skin was the color of a ghost's in the dim moonlight. When Pickering had tried to talk to him then, he stammered on about how he couldn't believe whatever it was he'd seen. He just couldn't believe it.

Now, when Garrett asked him about it after Wayne had had a chance to calm down, the man somehow couldn't recall much of anything about that night. In fact, he even tried covering himself by saying that he hadn't gotten there until the deputies had already started herding people away.

Since it had been Garrett who told the deputies to do that, he knew that Wayne was lying.

Donald Parker was another one with a similar story. Despite the fact that Garrett had spotted the elderly man staring out his window from his home directly across the street from Judge Fountain, Parker swore to Garrett's face that not only hadn't he seen anything, but he hadn't heard anything either. Since there were more bullet holes in the Fountains' house for Garrett to bother counting, he knew damn well that a man would have to be deaf to not hear a single one of them.

Garrett's biggest setback was when he'd gone to talk to Senator Avery. The very man who'd insisted on appointing him county sheriff answered Garrett's first question with a wide-eyed shake of his head and a blustering exhale.

"Sorry, Pat," the senator had said. "I wish I could help you, but it was a dark night. A lot going on. I put you on the job because I know you're the sort of man who keeps his head in situations like that. Me? Well, I'm a man who sits behind a desk."

Even though he knew there was a lot more that needed to be said, both on his and the senator's parts, Garrett knew the words were not going to be spoken. The senator had his reasons, whatever they might have been, and Garrett had his. Mainly, Garrett bit his tongue because the things he wanted to say wouldn't have done any good except to get the senator's feathers ruffled and that wouldn't help anyone.

Garrett went through the motions of talking to everyone else he could think of that had been there that night, but didn't come up with anything useful. Once he was convinced that they were covering someone's tracks, Garrett was only half listening to the witnesses' halfhearted excuses and flat-out lies anyway. He could already feel his blood starting to boil at the senseless walls that had been built against him by the very people he was trying to protect.

The more he thought about it, the worse it hit him inside, so Garrett tried to only think about the next steps he should take to make some progress in this case. The most he could hope for was that Adams wasn't running into the same kind of obstacles as he.

Since Garrett knew that Clint would be heading back to the sheriff's office, he headed that way after he was through talking to the last witness on his mental list. As always, Pickering was sitting with his feet propped up on his desk, flipping through the day's edition of the newspaper.

"Good day to ya, Pat," the sheriff said as Garrett walked inside. "What brings a man of your importance this way?"

"Just came by to check in on your prisoner."

Pickering set his paper down with deliberate slowness and carefully put his feet down on the floor one at a time. When he was done with that, he made a show out of getting up from his chair, moving as though he was a man at least thirty years older than he truly was. Finally, after shuffling around his desk, the sheriff made his way toward the door in the back of the room that led to the small row of jail cells.

"What happened to you, Pat?"

Garrett stopped and looked at the sheriff. Pickering glanced back at him with one hand resting on the door handle and the other hooked to his gun belt.

"It's only been a day since all this happened," Garrett said as the fatigue began creeping back into his voice.

"I know that, but a whole lot has changed since then, hasn't it?"

"I guess so."

"You've changed, too. All I want to know is why. What happened to you?"

Over the last several years, Garrett had developed a part of him that helped him deal with all the things people would say when they found out who he was. Ever since he'd been forced to put down William Bonney, Garrett had been called every name in the book by people that should have known better than to take the side of a murdering kid with a price on his head.

That part of Garrett was like an endless pit in the center of his mind where he could toss all those names and comments and they would disappear from his senses. He could block out the words and glance over all the newspaper articles that struck at the very heart of his character. But every so often, some of those words would lodge in Garrett's gut like a piece of meat that hadn't been chewed enough. It got stuck inside of him before getting chucked into the pit that could normally swallow it whole.

This was one of those times.

"You want to know what happened to me?" Garrett asked to the man who had, until this day, at least treated him with a measure of respect. "*This* is what happened to me." With that, Garrett pulled open his coat to show the county sheriff's badge hanging like a single star amid a clear black field of satin.

With his other hand, Garrett reached out and grabbed hold of the front of the sheriff's shirt, pulling him forward so fast that Pickering almost lost his footing. "I'm through with sitting by and trying not to listen to all the things people say about me. And I'm through with being treated like a stray dog just because you've passed judgment on me about something that you don't know a goddamn thing about. You can think what you want and you can say what you want behind my back because lord knows you're too yellow to say it to my face. But if you want to start pulling shit like this on me because you got your nose bent out of shape about suddenly being outranked by someone you thought was below you, then you'd best get over it and I mean fast."

Pickering's eyes narrowed and he reached up to pull Garrett's hand away, but was unable to budge the other man's grip.

Suddenly, the arrogant look on his face began to fade and the corner of one eye started to twitch.

This time, when Sheriff Pickering spoke, his voice was meeker. "Take it easy, Pat. All I was tryin' to do was—"

"I know what you were trying to do," Garrett said, ignoring the pair of deputies that were closing in behind him. "You were trying to get in the way of the sheriff of Dona Ana County in the middle of an investigation. And one more thing . . . I told you the other night that if you talked to me like that again, I'd put you on your ass."

Garrett twisted at the waist in a sharp semi-circle, pulling the sheriff along as he went. The motion took Pickering off guard and when he tried to adjust his feet beneath him, his body was already beginning to fall. Snapping with both wrists, Garrett tossed Pickering aside and was through the door to the jail before he hit the floor.

To his surprise, Clint was already standing at the end of the row, looking at him as though he was about to come running down the narrow aisle.

"What was all that about?" Clint asked.

"Just taking care of something that's been put aside for too long," Garrett replied. "Have you already had a chance to talk to Drezdev?"

Clint stood back so that Garrett could walk past him and look into the cells for himself. "That's not going to be as easy as we'd thought."

Garrett clenched his teeth together when he saw that the only people inside the jail were himself and Clint. The cells were all empty.

THIRTY-SIX

For a second or two, Clint and Garrett stood in silence looking at the empty cells. A constant flow of thoughts ran through Clint's mind and none of them reflected too well upon Sheriff Pickering. Also, along with all the accusations and conclusions, there was an underlying emotion that tainted Clint's innards all the way down to the marrow inside his bones.

Futility.

"What the hell are we doing here?" Garrett said, as though he could hear the frustration coursing through his deputy's mind. "Why the hell would—"

Garrett stopped himself, slammed a fist against one of the nearby iron bars and spun himself around so that he was facing the door to Pickering's office. He started to march straight back toward where the town's sheriff was waiting, his face a grim mask of deadly determination.

Reaching out with one hand, Clint grabbed hold of Garrett's elbow and pulled him back just before he'd made it to the door.

"Get your hands off me, Clint," Garrett seethed. "That's an order."

Clint stepped around so that he could look Garrett directly in the eyes. It was hard for most men to meet the lawman's intense stare, but Clint was one of the few that had the inner strength to keep from blinking no matter what was coming his way. "Think about what you're going to do, Pat. No matter how much you might want to, confronting Pickering isn't going to do anybody any good. Not right now."

Garrett's voice was made of cold iron forged from the cauldron blazing behind his eyes. "Drezdev should be here. There isn't a chance in hell that he was let out of here legally. So that means he was set free illegally. You know that just as well as I do."

"Of course I do. But if Pickering didn't want you to see that, he wouldn't have let either of us back here. He's probably standing out there right now waiting for you to make a move so he could justify pulling that badge off and throwing it in your face."

Something in what Clint said struck a chord within Garrett. The difference inside him only showed as a slight cooling of the fires that had been stoked inside him, but the difference was there nonetheless. Noticing this, Clint let go of Garrett's arm and stepped back.

Nodding, Garrett said, "You're right. Thanks, Clint." He took a deep breath and let it out, all while doing his best not to look at the vacant cells. "Drezdev may be free, but he hasn't been for long."

"Wherever he went, odds are that he's being slowed down from dragging a wounded man along with him."

"Krow?"

Clint nodded and proceeded to tell Garrett about what he'd seen at the doctor's office as well as his conversation with Hartnell. He also told him about being followed. Garrett took it all in while running his finger over his thick mustache.

"You checked the beds just to make sure?" he asked finally.

"There were only two patients in the place," Clint said. "One of them was too short to be Krow. I looked the other one in the face. It wasn't him."

"And this man you saw that was following you. Did you get a look at his face?"

"From the other end of an alley, but yes. It could have been Deacon, but then again it could have been anyone."

"Then it was Deacon. That one's survived this long because

he knows how to be forgotten once folks pass him by. He's not the sharpest knife in the drawer, but he knows when to lay low, which is something that a surprising number of outlaws just can't seem to get through their heads."

Garrett turned once again toward the office door, but without all of the fire that had caused Clint to stand in his way. "Looks like on top of everything else, we've got another man to track down. The way this is going, the only good thing is that once we find one, we'll probably find them all."

"Judge Fountain included?"

Pausing with his hand on the door's handle, Garrett took a moment to think that over. "We'll see."

When the door came open, Clint could see Sheriff Pickering standing with his hands on his hips, waiting for them both to emerge with a smug grin on his face. Once Garrett stepped aside, Clint spotted the other two deputies on duty waiting near the front door, hands resting on the butts of their guns.

"Find what you were looking for?" Pickering asked.

This time, when Garrett approached him, Pickering seemed ready for whatever the other man was set to do. His eyes glared defiantly and he wrapped his fist around his pistol, stopping right before clearing leather.

But rather than lay a finger on Pickering, Garrett stood toe to toe with him and stared him down until he wore away some of the edge in the other man's gaze. Clint walked through the room toward the front door. The deputies there stood their ground without budging . . . right up to the moment when Clint walked right up and reached in between them as though they weren't even there.

Grudgingly, the two deputies moved aside, trying to keep their dignity by not looking away while they stepped back. All they managed to do was show Clint just how nervous they were and how much they wished both he and Garrett would just hurry up and leave.

Once Garrett heard the front door opening on hinges that were in need of some oil, he allowed the grim line of his mouth to curve into a subtle grin. "I've said everything I needed to say to you already, Pickering. Everything except this . . . fuck you."

With that still hanging in the air over Pickering's head like a small black cloud, Garrett turned his back on the other lawman and strode out the door. Clint stepped out next and let the door slam shut behind him.

Garrett took a couple steps outside until he was standing on the edge of the boardwalk looking out over the street. He placed his hands on his hips and scanned the area as though he'd just pulled into town and was seeing it for the first time. When he turned around to face Clint, he was still wearing the same smile that he'd put on especially for Sheriff Pickering.

"You know something?" Garrett said. "For the first time in a while, I feel good. No . . . not just good. *Damn* good."

Looking at the newest sheriff of Dona Ana County, Clint didn't see a man behind a badge or even the man who'd put an end to Billy the Kid. What he saw was just a man who'd finally gotten a measure of satisfaction after waiting patiently for too many years.

"I'll bet you do, Pat."

THIRTY-SEVEN

Stepping down off the boardwalk and into the street, Pat Garrett seemed like a man transformed. His eyes were focused on the road ahead, seeing nothing but the goal he was working toward and the steps that needed to be taken to get there.

Clint walked beside him as all of the pieces to the puzzle revolving around Judge Fountain swirled in his head. They were coming together to form a more coherent picture, even though the last piece they'd been given seemed to tear everything they'd done apart. With Drezdev gone, that meant that Sheriff Pickering was somehow involved in the judge's disappearance.

Clint's first thought had been that Pickering must be crooked and in league with Drezdev. But then a small, seemingly insignificant piece of the puzzle clicked into the right spot inside Clint's brain, making everything else make just a little more sense. He didn't have the proof just yet to back up everything he was thinking, but judging by the determined strength in Garrett's stride, now was the time to get things done . . . not sit around trying to double-check every last notion.

They were heading back to the Fountain home as though they were dead certain that they were not going to be there alone. Every step they took down the street was made with supreme confidence. By the time they were less than a block away from the part of town with the biggest houses and most influential families, Garrett had reached down to flip the leather thong from his holster that had been holding his gun in place.

"There's something at that house that will give us the rest of the answers we need," he said to Clint. "You look for it and I'll cover you."

Nodding, Clint asked, "So you're getting that feeling too, huh?"

"The one where you think you're being watched?"

"That'd be the one."

"No," Garrett said. "I *know* we're being watched. If Deacon's in town, there hasn't been enough blood spilled for him to leave just yet. He's waiting to take his shot at one or both of us. It's his way. Whether he knows we're onto him or not, it won't matter. He's had a taste of blood and he won't leave until he's had his fill."

They were in sight of the house. It stood alone and empty in its lot like the shell of a giant dead animal. It still had all the outward appearances it had had when it was full of life, but it had since been scooped out and was rotting where it lay. Devoid of life. Drawing the maggots to pick away at what little it had left to offer.

Clint was getting that same feeling again. Except this time it was screaming inside of him to watch out for the shot that would be coming at any second. Now that he knew what to look for, there was no need for the furtive glances over his shoulder or the cautious side trips down alleys.

His reflexes were at peak performance and were ready to snap him into action if there was so much as a hint of Deacon Hobbs coming from any direction.

Also, his mind was no longer distracted by trying to figure out what had happened that night when the Fountain murders had taken place. There were no more questions in Clint's mind about what had happened. No more uncertainty as to what it was he was looking for. Like Garrett, Clint didn't *think* anything anymore.

He *knew*.

The front of the house loomed before them like a shattered

facade. Broken windows, swinging door, bloodstained wood
and all. Rather than go over the details he'd seen a thousand
times once again, Clint went straight inside the house and stood
next to a worn, comfortable-looking chair that might have been
the judge's favorite.

Garrett stood in the doorway, keeping an eye on the street
while also observing what Clint was doing.

Clint stood in the spot where he figured the judge had been
standing at the moment Deacon Hobbs and his accomplice had
entered the Fountain home. Scanning the room in the revealing
light of day, Clint saw details scattered about that made him
certain of his final theory as to what had happened.

"Deacon works by keeping a low profile and blending in with
the surroundings," Clint said. "So that means he would have
come in through the front door. It's the quickest and least com-
plicated way."

"At the very least, Fountain would have opened the door to
talk to the man," Garrett agreed. "That was his style."

"And, considering that all he needed to do was open the door
enough for Deacon to charge inside, that really wouldn't have
been too hard. Since Deacon is a hired killer, we have to assume that it wasn't his idea to take away Fountain's boy."

Garrett thought about that for a second and shook his head.
"He's never bothered with kidnapping before. Killing's a
quicker job and the money's better."

"So that means that someone hired him for the job, but the
thing that's been bothering me is why someone would go
through so much trouble and then not even leave a note behind
as to what his demands are, how much he wants, or anything
of the sort."

Taking a step inside the house, Garrett looked around in the
illuminating daylight and found the same thing that Clint had
seen upon entering. In the corner, there was a smaller chair on
rockers situated next to a pile of blocks, and a small chalkboard.
When they'd both seen that place before, they knew there were
traces of blood, but now they could see something else alto-
gether.

What had before looked like some blood spilled on a dark
floor by the light of a sputtering lantern could now be seen for

what it was: a patch of blood that was soaked into the floor so badly that it had turned the wood black. More importantly, the rocker itself was coated with a similar layer of gore that had made the entire chair look like it was made out of stained lumber in the terrible lighting of the night before. What stained the wood wasn't varnish, but enough blood to prove a much more gruesome point than just the scattered stains that had been pointed out before.

"Sheriff Pickering was the one who sent for you, right?"

Garrett nodded.

"And I don't suppose he looked too closely at this while you were here?" Clint asked, pointing toward the blood-soaked chair and floor.

Garret shook his head. "No. The light was so dim that I thought the chair might have just been painted black."

Clint looked back and forth from the chair to the floor and to the broken window, picturing the set of footprints he knew was outside. "There's only one way all of this can fit together," Clint stated simply. "The boy who sat in that chair was shot and killed. There's no way someone that size could bleed out that much and live very long. I've seen enough gunshot wounds to know that much. So that leaves the judge, himself."

"I can tell you one thing for sure. If folks around here would lie and cover up for anyone it would be for Judge Fountain. That means he must've done something that needed covering. All that's left is the rest of this blood that's around the window and floor."

"The judge saw his boy in danger, got his hands on a gun and—"

"Acted on instinct," came a voice from the back of the house. "Nothing more."

Clint and Garrett turned toward the sound and almost went for their guns. They stopped when they saw the dirty, disheveled face of Judge Fountain lurking in the shadows as though he was haunting his own living room.

The judge looked at the two men and then his eyes drifted over to the empty rocker and stayed there. In a dry, rasping voice he said, "Any father would've done the same."

THIRTY-EIGHT

Judge Fountain looked as though he belonged in the coffin that was waiting for him at the funeral parlor. Although folks in town had been hoping to hear otherwise, it had been the general opinion that the judge and his son were already dead. By the faraway look in his eyes and the pasty hue to his skin, Judge Fountain himself was of that same opinion.

Although Clint had been surprised to hear the judge's voice at that particular moment, he wasn't so shocked to see the man up and around. "Glad you didn't make us come looking for you, Judge," Clint said.

Fountain stayed in the shadows at the back of the room. In the space of a day, he seemed to have dwindled down to half his size as he stood hunched in a corner like he could barely stand. "I've been with ... friends. They said you two were looking for me, although they really didn't expect you to get so close so quickly."

"Senator Avery doesn't have much faith in me, does he?" Garrett asked.

The judge stared silently ahead for a moment and then looked up to meet Garrett's eyes. "No, Pat. He didn't. Actually, he put you on the job for that very reason. I'm sorry."

Garrett was unaffected by the news. In fact, he nodded curtly as though it wasn't even news to him at all. "And the rest of the people who saw what happened . . . they covered for you as well?"

"Yes. They were kind enough to help me out, but I couldn't accept their help if it was going to get them in any trouble. That would be too selfish for me to do, no matter what the reason."

"I don't know about that," Clint said. "Killing a man seems like a pretty good reason to me."

Clint spoke those words with a frankness that cut right down to the heart of the matter. Waiting to see what kind of reaction he would get, Clint watched the judge turn his face back toward the floor as the shadows seemed to darken all around him. Fountain's expression told Clint that he'd been completely right about what had happened. Although there was a small sense of victory inside Clint's mind, it was tempered by the fact that he had to be right about a tragedy such as this one.

"That wasn't any of the killers who jumped out the window, was it, Judge?" Clint asked. "It was you. You were the one going out that way and it was you who was carrying out a body."

Judge Fountain's silence spoke volumes. Rather than say anything for or against Clint's statements, he simply kept his head down and stared at the small rocker.

Taking a step forward, Clint went on. "You saw those men come into your house and threaten your boy."

Fountain nodded.

"What did they want from you?" Garrett asked.

"They . . . they knocked on my door and said they wanted to talk to me about a grand jury case I was working on. They said it was important and couldn't wait until the morning. I see a lot of folks that way, but there was something about the man who was doing the talking. I never saw him before."

Judge Fountain took a breath and leaned back against the wall, suddenly needing it for support. "I started to shut the door, but the one in front pushed it open and knocked me back. That was when I saw the face of the one behind him." As the memories started rushing back, Fountain's eyes became wide and he looked around as if he was seeing a ghostly vision of that terrible night.

"It was Will Krow. He was bandaged up and could barely walk, but he came into my home behind the first one and shut the door behind him. The other man grabbed Henry . . . my poor Henry . . ."

The way Judge Fountain was staring at the rocker, Clint knew that Henry must have been his son. It wasn't until that moment that Clint was able to put a name to the dead child's memory.

Snapping himself out of his nightmare, Fountain looked up at Garrett and then at Clint. "He took Henry and told me how I was to rule on a cattle rustling case that's in the process of being heard. That was when Krow stepped in and also told me I needed to have Mick Drezdev set free just like I did with you, Mister Adams.

"They put a gun to Henry's head and said they'd shoot if I didn't swear to do these things." Fountain paused to take a deep breath, which he swallowed as if the air was water going into a parched throat. "Of course I agreed, but they were going to take him anyway. They called it insurance." Anger flared inside the judge's eyes. Gritting his teeth, he clenched his fists and rasped, "My Henry was nothing but insurance." The rage subsided enough for him to fight back the emotions and continue with his account. "After that, I don't know what happened, really. The stranger grabbed Henry and headed for the door while Krow stayed behind with his gun pointed at me. I—I tried to get him to give my son back, but they wouldn't listen. I tried to run after him, but Krow pushed me back. When he put his hands on me and shoved me down . . . I saw . . . red." The anger returned, bubbling inside Fountain like a pool of lava. "I took a swing at him and knocked him back. He probably didn't see that coming from a man of my years. The next thing I knew, I grabbed the gun from his hand and started walking for the door. That was when the other one looked back in and aimed his pistol as though he was going to shoot. I thought I was going to die and never see my boy again. That was when he threw Henry down and came at me. Henry ran inside and . . . and hid behind his chair. I guess he felt safe there."

At this point, Fountain held up his hands, which were still shaking as though they still bore the weight of the gun he'd been holding. "Krow held back . . . since he was wounded . . . and the stranger aimed his gun at me and then . . . at Henry. He said something, but I don't remember what . . . something about both of us dying. I didn't want my boy hurt and I was about to toss the gun down, but I guess it wasn't fast enough for him."

All the anger that had been inside Fountain, all of the rage, turned into sorrow and spilled out of him as tears started rolling down his face. "There was a shot . . . and I thought I was dead. But it wasn't me that was hit . . . it was my boy . . . my Henry who fell over his chair and it was his blood that poured all over it. When I saw that . . . I started shooting. I shot at the stranger, who was standing by the door, and the stranger shot back at me. But Krow was in the way and I stayed behind him so I wouldn't be hit. As much as I wanted to die right then, I couldn't get myself to stand in front of a bullet. All I could think about was my son and all I could see was his blood. I fired again and again until finally Krow looked at me and . . . he . . . smiled." Pausing again, Fountain wiped away his tears and straightened his back. "My last shot went through his face. I stared down at him when he dropped and when I looked up, I saw people standing outside looking in. The stranger was gone, so I carried Krow out the window and I buried him. Then I carried Henry away and buried him as well . . . in a spot outside of town where we used to go sometimes."

Clint stepped forward to try and comfort the judge, but it was Garrett who put his hand on Fountain's shoulder and led him out of the room. All three of them went into the small dining room at the back of the house. Furnished with a finely polished oak table and a mahogany cabinet in one corner, the room was a stark contrast to the bloody mess in the room they'd just left.

Garrett helped the judge sit down in one of four wooden chairs.

"Senator Avery is a good friend of mine," Fountain said after catching his breath. "Along with the rest of my neighbors. He said he saw what happened and that I shouldn't be ashamed of killing the son of a bitch that murdered my Henry. He . . . helped me bury Krow and the others who saw what I did agreed not to speak of it. Since I'm a judge working on federal as well as some local cases, I couldn't just leave town. I was to hide out for a while and head east when things died down. The senator wanted to cover my tracks by starting an investigation that would never be solved."

"And that's where I came in," Garrett said.

"I didn't want you involved in this, Pat. I swear. I even had Drezdev released like I'd promised so that they might just leave town. That stranger was the only one who knows what happened who might see to it that it comes out. That would only ruin my reputation and I'd never be able to come back. More than likely, I'd be wanted for murder."

"But it was self-defense," Clint said. "You've got plenty of witnesses to speak for you."

"Sure I do. Witnesses that already lied to the town sheriff and tried to help me escape from the law. The federal case I'm working on is a dispute between some powerful people. People who would pay to finish the job Krow and that stranger had started. Whatever happens with my trial, it will only make it easier for those men to find me and silence me for good. Either way . . . whether I'm hung for murder or shot for doing my job . . . I'm a dead man."

THIRTY-NINE

Clint had listened to every word the judge had said. For the most part, his story had meshed with what he'd been thinking after piecing together the things he'd seen. As far as the federal case Fountain had mentioned, Clint figured he might as well take the judge's word for it since he didn't make it a habit to keep up on such things.

All this time, Clint had known that there was something that just didn't fit in what Pickering and the others had been telling him. That, combined with the way Garrett had been treated by the law and locals alike, made everything about the Fountain murders seem somewhat . . . off. After all, why would a two-bit killer like Drezdev take it upon himself to kill a judge? Now, after having it all laid out in front of him, Clint could see that Drezdev had been the one who had been used.

Whether or not he'd contacted Deacon, Drezdev was merely an excuse for the real killer to use so he could get close enough to Fountain. In fact, Clint was certain now that the judge was lucky to be alive at all and now that he'd come out of hiding . . .

Clint's head snapped up as every one of his instincts blared inside his head. "Who else knows that you're over here, Judge Fountain?" Clint asked as he stepped over to a window and looked carefully outside.

"I was at the house across the street and when I saw you two come in here I snuck over and came in through the back. I'm not sure if anyone saw me."

Looking over to Garrett, Clint said, "Only if they were watching the house already."

Garrett understood immediately what Clint was saying and hurried toward the back door. "Damn! If Deacon was following you, then he's probably been outside the whole time. We've got to get the judge out of here."

Looking between the two men, Judge Fountain wore a confused expression on his weary face. "What are you talking about? Who's Deacon?"

"Deacon was the man hired to kill you, sir," Garrett explained. "He's the stranger who shot Henry."

"But I haven't seen him since that night. Nobody has."

"Did anyone get a good look at his face?"

"Some of the neighbors said they did, but . . ."

"That's what Deacon does," Garrett said. "He lays low until he's found his man. Waits for him to show himself and then he moves in."

Realizing what he'd done, Fountain pushed himself away from the table, got to his feet and held his hand out. "One of you, give me a gun. I started this and I won't have any more people getting hurt on my behalf."

Clint pushed Fountain back into his seat with one hand, while pulling aside the curtain of a small window with his other. "There's no need for that. Whether he thought we could do it or not, Senator Avery gave us a job to do. Now it's time to finish it."

"Is he out there?" Fountain asked.

Garrett carefully looked outside, making sure not to move too far away from what little cover the door would provide. "He's out there. Clint's spotted him around town, which means he's not leaving until he's found you."

Suddenly, there was a loud rattling sound coming from the front room. It was the door scraping across the floor after being pulled from one of its hinges. The noise sounded like the shuffling of a stool being dragged across uneven wooden planks and was accompanied by the high shriek of the one remaining hinge.

Clint turned toward the doorway that led from the dining room to the front room, making sure to position himself in front of Judge Fountain. Footsteps clomped into the house, echoing through the rooms and bouncing off the walls. Glancing toward the back door, Clint motioned for Garrett to check outside. Garrett nodded, drew his gun and slowly opened the back door.

The footsteps sounded as though they were coming from all sides. It was at that moment that Clint realized there wasn't one person coming, but two from opposite ends of the house. Before Clint could say a word of warning, he saw a figure pounce in front of Garrett from where it had been waiting just outside the house. A quick blur flashed toward Garrett, followed by the sickening crunch of metal slamming into flesh and bone.

Clint was already in the motion of drawing when he heard the second set of footsteps from the living room speed up into a pounding rush. He was able to reverse the direction of his turn just in time to see Drezdev come running into the room, his gun already drawn and ready to fire.

There were shots coming from the back of the room, but Clint was too busy to see what Garrett was doing. Instead, he was barely able to move quick enough to get to Drezdev before the outlaw pulled his trigger. Clint threw himself forward and grabbed hold of the other man who came at him like a freight train.

With his left hand, Clint grabbed hold of Drezdev's wrist while burying his right deep into the outlaw's stomach. He was just able to pull Drezdev's gun toward the ceiling before it went off and sent a bullet into the wood over their heads. With the gunshot rattling inside his ears, Clint punched Drezdev again, doubling the outlaw over so he could send a knee into the killer's chin.

Drezdev grunted once as he choked up a lungful of air. He nearly dropped to the floor, but he quickly got his wits about him and struggled to get his gun arm free from Clint's grasp. Turning his upper body quickly to one side, he buried an elbow into Clint's ribs and managed to break his right hand away.

Pain shot through Clint's body as the impact of Drezdev's elbow drove like a spike into his chest. Ignoring the pain, he pulled his right hand down tight against his body and then snapped it out into a powerful uppercut that sent Drezdev reeling back a few steps.

The outlaw brought his hand up to his face as blood began pouring out from between his fingers. He tried to take aim, but for the moment, his hand was shaking too badly to draw a bead on much of anything besides the floor or one of the nearby walls.

Clint spun around to look at what the judge was doing. When he looked at where he'd left the other man, he saw nothing but an overturned chair and a body laying on the floor. At first, he thought Fountain had been hit, but then he saw the judge pull himself under the table.

When he turned around again, Clint was barely able to get his hands up in front of his face before the butt of Drezdev's gun came sailing toward him. This time, Clint's forearm caught Drezdev's wrist along the bottom where he impacted against the nerves running through the killer's arm. Drezdev howled in pain and his fingers opened up in a reflex caused by Clint's blow. His gun rattled to the floor and landed at Clint's feet.

Clint ignored the pistol for the moment and sent a vicious right cross into Drezdev's jaw. He could see the lights dim behind Drezdev's eyes, but still followed up with another left hook, which all but removed the other man's head at the shoulders.

Drezdev staggered forward and then teetered back, moving his arms as though he was still trying to put up a fight. Just then, a gunshot blasted through the room like a cannon.

Clint threw himself to the floor since the gunshot had come from directly behind him and reached for the Colt at his side. At the same time, he looked to see who'd fired and found Judge Fountain crouched beside the table, holding Drezdev's smoking pistol in both hands.

When he saw the look in Fountain's eyes, Clint spun around to face Drezdev. The outlaw was still standing the way he'd left him, balancing on his feet like a doll almost set to fall. Except this time, there was a black, gaping hole where his left

eye had been and a trickle of blood ran down his cheek like
dark crimson tears.

Finally, the killer dropped.

Judge Fountain let the gun fall from his hand.

Clint didn't waste another moment with Drezdev. Instead, he
rushed to the back door where Garrett had been standing only
moments before. The lawman was no longer there and the door
leading outside swung back and forth as a figure crouched on
one knee outside.

Clint made his way carefully to the back door. He tried to
think of how many shots he'd heard coming from outside, but
knew he'd been too busy to know for sure. Since Deacon made
his living by his gun, Clint knew it was safe to assume that he
hadn't gone through all of his ammunition yet.

When he looked through the door, Clint saw a scene that
was very familiar.

Standing outside with his hands at his side, was the same
man he'd seen earlier that day at the other end of the alley.
Clint looked at the figure on the porch and found Pat Garrett
with a hand clamped over a bloody patch on his left shoulder.

"I'm all right," Garrett said before Clint could ask. Besides
the wound in his shoulder, Garrett's face was covered in blood
that had been smeared over his skin like a savage's war paint.

"Glad to see you made it out here," Deacon said from his
position roughly twenty feet away. "I was waiting so I could
get the both of you together. After today . . . I'm gonna be a
famous man."

FORTY

Deacon Hobbs stood with his hands hanging down at his sides. He waited there with a smug grin on his face, reflecting the confidence that flowed from his every pore. Stubble covered his face and his clothes hung on his body, shielding just about every inch of the man from plain sight. All that remained of him that wasn't covered in clothing, hair or hat was his eyes.

There was no hiding the eyes.

Clint stared into those eyes, knowing that they were all he had to see if he was going to beat this man. He'd never seen Deacon in action and wasn't even sure if he was very fast, but he wasn't about to catch a bullet because he'd underestimated an enemy.

Garrett stood at Clint's side, armed yet nursing his wounds. From personal experience, Clint knew that a wound in the right place could slow any man down just enough to get himself killed. He had every faith in Garrett's skill and intention, but he was unsure as to just how well the lawman could function under the circumstances.

So, the only person Clint could count on was himself. He was in familiar territory.

Just then, Deacon's posture slumped forward a bit. He let his chin sag and he brought his hands up to waist level. "I've

181

heard all about you, Garrett," Deacon said. "I know you're here to kill me. That's what you do, isn't it?"

None of his wounds were reflected in Garrett's voice. He spoke in cool, even tones that betrayed not even the slightest amount of discomfort. "I'm here to take you in. Throw down your guns and I'll see you get to your cell alive."

Listening to Deacon speak, Clint didn't believe a word that came out of his mouth. As he watched the killer raise his hands, Clint caught the glint of sunlight reflected from a sliver of metal poking out from behind one of Deacon's fingers.

In a motion that was almost too fast to see, Deacon flicked his wrists and snapped a Derringer into each hand. He brought up the weapons as the grin on his face turned into a full-blown smile.

Clint's heart thumped once in his chest like a mallet against his ribs. Without taking his eyes off of Deacon, he reached for his Colt. A fraction of a second after his palm touched the familiar grip, he'd cleared leather and was already squeezing the trigger. At the exact moment he pointed the barrel at Deacon, Clint felt the gun buck in his hand to send a single piece of lead into its spiraling flight.

Clint's heart thumped once more just as his bullet drilled through Deacon's chest.

Time seemed to slow down for the next few moments as Deacon struggled to keep on his feet. The impact from Clint's bullet had hit him like a mule-kick, but something deep inside the man refused to let him drop. The harder he tried to fire the little guns that had been secreted up his sleeves, the more his body resisted.

Finally, the killer realized that he couldn't breathe.

He couldn't see or hear, either. Then, like the clock inside him had simply wound to a halt, Deacon Hobbs fell facefirst to the ground.

Clint walked over to the body and kicked the Derringers away from Deacon's hands just to be safe. When he looked back to the porch, he saw Garrett standing with gun in hand, ready to cover him if the need were to arise.

"I never saw anything so fast," Garrett said. "I almost don't believe it."

The Colt fit perfectly in Clint's hand as though it had been crafted to fit in that particular place. The weapon was a masterpiece of craftsmanship that had taken all of Clint's talents to improve. Looking down at it, he knew that if he'd had to take the extra fraction of a second to thumb back the hammer, it might very well have been him laying on the ground instead of Deacon. For that reason, he knew that Garrett had saved his life by making sure that the Colt was where it belonged when it was needed the most.

Sliding the Colt back into its holster, Clint walked over to Garrett and helped him into the house. "Did he have anyone else with him?" Clint asked.

"No," Garrett said with a wince as he lowered himself into one of the dining room chairs. "All I saw was him."

"There's no more of them," came a voice from the other side of the room.

Clint looked over and saw Judge Fountain standing over Drezdev's body. He looked down at the corpse as though he was waiting for the dead man to get up and walk away. "This was their chance," he said. "After today, they won't be able to get near me because I'll be in jail where I belong."

Garrett reached inside his jacket pocket and pulled out a white handkerchief. After cleaning some of the blood from his face, he looked over to Fountain and said, "What good would it do to put you in jail? You've been through more hell than any jail sentence could give. Besides, once you leave this town, you're no longer a problem of Dona Ana County or Sheriff Pickering." He got up and walked over to the judge. "Just put this behind you. Trust me, you'll have your whole life to live with the pain."

Judge Fountain looked at Garrett and then at Clint. Unable to find the proper words, he nodded to both men, walked through the back door and left his old life behind.

Clint watched as the door slammed shut behind the judge. Looking to Garrett, he said, "Do you think this is really over?"

"Deacon worked alone. He wouldn't have taken the job otherwise."

"Sounds like you knew him pretty well."

"I know his kind well enough." Garrett pulled himself up out of his chair and stepped over Drezdev's body. "Come on," he said. "Let's go tell Senator Avery the good news."

Watch for

THE SHADOW OF THE GUNSMITH

244th novel in the exciting GUNSMITH series
from Jove

Coming in April!

J. R. ROBERTS
THE GUNSMITH

LONGARM

Explore the exciting Old West with one of the men who made it wild!